Angry King

Ophelia Kee

OPHELIA KEE

Introduction

THE DRAOITHE SAGA BY OPHELIA KEE

Draoithe Saga

Steamy hot, wickedly delicious paranormal romance, magical realism, and urban fantasy stories set in a dream to live for!

Those who come to Draoithe aid in the fight to restore the magical balance of the dream, one couple at a time.

Grab a good drink, curl up in a good seat, choose a book from the Saga, and escape into the dream while you meet the men and women who call it home.

Draoithe is a world in which myths, legends, and fairytales walk among the strange and wonderful.

They often find balance in a lifemate, and the magic from the past lives again!

Welcome to the dream...

Steamy Urban Fantasy and Paranormal Romance Stories with Fated Mates 18+ HEA! NC!

***Warning: Adult Themes, Fantasy Violence, and/or Explicit Sexual Situations. Intended for a Mature Audience.

A Note from Ophelia Kee

Note to the Reader:

A saga is defined as a long story of heroic achievement, especially a medieval prose narrative often found in Old Norse or Old Icelandic. It's a form of the novel in which the members of a social group chronicle a long story detailing a dramatic history.

Compartmentalized in several miniseries for easier reading, the Draoithe Saga tells the story of the founding of an immortal kingdom in the Leaindeail to combat those responsible for unbalancing the magic of the dream. It's told through the eyes of those connected with its creation and the readers see the story through tales of couples who find hope through their connection to Draoithe.

The central time frame is the year 2016, although pertinent information from the past reveals itself as the characters understand it. The central place is an eerily familiar yet magical realist, Tyler, Texas. As the tale draws out, other kingdoms set in other locations interact with the Druid pack to bring about the end of Peter Elliot and restore the balance of magic, so those tales, too, became a part of the Draoithe Saga as well. Cameo appearances of characters from other tales are common. Overlapping scenes from the events often relates alternate perspectives as the story unfolds.

Watch the trailer, research videos, vlogs, and more on YouTube.

Subscribe to Ophelia Kee on YouTube

Story Description

Angry King

Royal Council Volume 4

A Draoithe Saga Tale

Is his anger enough to face an invincible enemy?

Enyeto Locklear, Griz, was both a bear of a man and a grizzly bear shifter. Born with both sides of the dream magic, he could walk through the dream and step onto the path in the stillness and see possible futures. Marked for kidnapping and poisoned at a bar is where the nightmare which led to his death began. Only he can't remember what happened. Discovering the truth about his near death experience intertwines in the surprise meeting of the woman he would love.

Melody Brooks is a young snowy owl shifter. She first encountered her mate, Griz, in a picturesque dream. When things changed and he begged her for help in a twisted nightmare which stole her sleep, she did the unimaginable, and stole him from himself. Unable to discover his location on her own, she sought aid from the immortals at Draoithe.

Melody may have saved Griz from a fate worse than death, but she also altered him in ways he found difficult to understand. With his magic changed and a past he couldn't remember, his frustration mounted over his weakened state until it was only a matter of time before things exploded.

Melody needed her mate and a safe place to call home. Prophesied to be the seventh king, Griz would be the last member of the Royal Council at Draoithe. But before Griz could claim his mate and take his place as the seventh king of Draoithe, he needed a reckoning, and the ones responsible for it all had to pay.

Angry King is an urban fantasy with steamy paranormal romance, and the last tale in the Royal Council, a Draoithe Saga miniseries by Ophelia Kee. If you love come-back-from-the-brink and utterly-destroy-the-enemy fantasy tales where the hero gets the girl and the crown, Angry King is your next intense read.

It's more than a story; it's an experience. Welcome to the dream...

Urban Fantasy with Steamy Paranormal Romance and Fated Mates 18+ HEA! NC!

***Warning: Adult Themes, Fantasy Violence, and/or Explicit Sexual Situations. Intended for a Mature Audience.

Character Introduction

Melody Brooks

Melody Brooks was a fashion design college grad. But her career hadn't taken off, and she worked hard at a dead end nowhere job, barely getting by when a grizzly bear invaded her dreams. He was big and scary, but he was nice to her. When he disappeared, then called her to him from a sinister warehouse, she knew she had to get help. Her need to rescue him led her to seek Fox at Draoithe and to find her mate.

Melody Brooks

ANGRY KING

AKA: snowbird

Smells like: gardenia

Owner and Fashion designer for Immortal Outfitters

Mate: Griz

White hair with blonde streaks

Golden eyes

5'1" tall

110 lbs

26 years old

Snowy Owl-submissive

Melody wants Griz, but she also wants to continue her career as a fashion designer. Draoithe makes her an offer she can't refuse. If she can convince Griz to stay, she could have it all.

Enyeto Locklear

Enyeto Locklear is a grizzly bear shifter who was born with both sides of the dream walker gift. Abducted from his favorite bar in Boulder, Colorado, by three evil dragons and forced to endure medical experiments at the hands of Peter Elliot's evil minions, the six feet four inch bear of a man is aided by Luke and the dragons of Draoithe because his life mate sought help after stealing his consciousness.

Enyeto Locklear

AKA: Griz

Smells like: baled hay in the sun.

Manager of Bear Necessities Organic Farm

Mate: Melody

Brown eyes

Dark brown hair

6'4" tall

260 lbs

112 years old

Dreamwalker/Grizzly bear- Alpha

Griz enjoys working outdoors and prefers a hands-on-approach to things, including handmade furniture. Finding Melody in the dream saved him, and following her will change the course of his life. He seeks a reckoning and to join the Druid pack.

Contents

Newsletter Friends

Magic Scroll

ANGRY KING

Dear Reader,
Angry King is the finale for the Royal Council Miniseries.
I hope you enjoyed it all.
For more information, please join my group of
Newsletter Friends

Newsletter Friends

Welcome to the dream...

Note To The Reader

Note to the reader

Angry King follows the tales of Vampire Knight, Dream Walker, Vampire Panther, and Quest for the Valkyries in the Draoithe Saga timeline. The events in this story occur simultaneously with the events recorded in the Valkyries Ride miniseries. This tale, like most of the stories in the Draoithe Saga, is not a stand-alone story. For the best reading experience, the author recommends reading the Kingdom Rising miniseries, followed by the Royal Council miniseries. Angry King is the finale for the Royal Council miniseries. Thank you for supporting an independent author. Welcome to the dream...

-OK

Prologue

Griz

When Griz woke, he found her asleep in his arms. How did that happen?

He dragged his attention away from the snowy owl that slept in his arms and looked around the room. Griz didn't know where he was.

Wherever he was, the bed was comfortable. He turned his attention back to the snowbird that was snoring softly next to his heart.

The last thing Griz remembered from the waking world was being in that warehouse. He knew the owl, but he didn't know her name, did he?

He'd only ever seen her in her animal form in the dream. Her white hair struck him. It had single dark blond strands scattered through it.

He touched it. The light floral scent of *gardenia* that he knew to belong to the owl in his dream drifted to him strongly as he felt her hair.

He shouldn't be touching her hair. He didn't know the woman. They'd never met, and yet there she was asleep in his arms in the waking world.

Griz recognized her as his mate instantly. It puzzled him how she could be in his arms. None of it made sense.

He should try to rise and see where he was, but disturbing her sleep was out of the question. She enthralled him. He remained exactly as he was.

Griz was hungry. Between the damage done to him physically over the last two weeks and the dreamwalk with Kallik and Eli to heal the broken little arctic fox, he could eat enough to hibernate.

The snowy owl stole his awareness, and he needed to sleep more, as well.

His ankle hurt. Someone had splinted it, so it would heal properly. He needed to thank someone.

Had the snowy owl done that for him? Where had she come from? Would she return?

He wanted to rumble his displeasure at the idea she might leave, but he played with her soft white hair instead. He didn't want her to wake up. The dream would end then.

His world narrowed to only her. She was soft and warm asleep in his arms, and he lost himself in her. She was *everything*. Griz slept again...

CHAPTER ONE

Big Grouchy Grizzly Bear

*L*uke

Kallik sat in Fox's library with Andrei, Javier, Luke, and Fox. Late lunch was over. It was Sunday evening.

"I want to raise you as Ruiri. Are you interested?" Luke asked.

"Yes. Why?"

After what he'd seen at the warehouse, Kallik understood Luke's desire to build the council. He wanted to know why himself specifically.

Luke looked at Javier. Javier nodded and spoke.

"Because you think first and would choose peace if possible," Javier said.

"You came here seeking life and your mate. Help us defend what you desire to keep."

Andrei told him the truth as he had when Kallik first arrived.

"You need the pack to protect Mihaela, just as I need the pack to protect Artie. We're stronger together," Fox argued.

"You've more than proven your worth. We need you. It isn't a secret I wanted you on the council from the beginning. I waited for you to bond

1

with Mihaela for the balance. She would need to agree. Will you give me your decision by Wednesday?" Luke asked.

"Wednesday. I will speak with Mihaela and let you know."

Kallik didn't want to make a choice for his vampire consort and declined to answer right away.

"Thank you, Kallik," Luke said.

Kallik stood and grasped forearms with his alpha. The big man turned and left the library.

When the door closed, Javier spoke up.

"I want Ryker. He and Lily bonded. They're part of the pack. I think he would be good for the council."

"I want him, too," Fox said.

"Sure you aren't just partial because he helped save Artie?"

Luke grinned at his friend.

"She's everything to me, but no. It's because of the way he treats Lily," Fox said.

"Say it, Fox. He's not as stuffy and serious as I am."

Andrei laughed.

Ryker hadn't spent two hundred years hiding what he was. He was more open about his abilities because they were too new and no harm would come to him using them at Draoithe as long as he used them positively.

Andrei was far more formal. Two hundred years as the personal guard to the enclave's Princess had left its mark on Andrei.

"He had my vote already. We have an excellent history of working together in the military. I say Ryker next as well. Andrei, do you have anything against that idea?"

Luke waited for the newest member of the council's input.

"No, I agree with Fox. The man sees the world differently. He's a bit like Javier in that respect. His moral fiber is good. He moved away from

Sanchez and Elliot to seek an alternative. Lily killed him, and he's been stuck on her ever since. He's balanced and loyal. I say we offer him a far larger stake in the Leaindeail than he ever dreamed of."

Andrei smiled.

"Is it too fast?" Luke asked.

"Nah. Ryker won't see it that way. He'll just see it as the next step. He wanted to be here even before he turned into a vampire. Andrei is right about his willingness to accept the world simply as it is. It'll work," Javier said.

"He's a stray. I'm keeping him, so the question isn't whether he'll join the council, but when?" Fox said.

Luke rolled his eyes. Sometimes Fox was all Ruiri. He'd been born a Druid king, and five hundred years hadn't changed that.

"I cannot argue with Fox's choices in strays. Nadine is everything." Andrei grinned.

"First it was Javier and now you," Luke groaned.

Javier high-fived Fox, who grinned like the Cheshire cat.

"No time like the present, boss," Javier said.

"Shall I get him?"

Luke nodded. Javier texted Ryker. A few minutes later, Ryker teleported into the library. He'd been working in Eli's garage, adding window tinting to all the vehicles the pack accumulated.

The sun hadn't set yet. Teleportation was an extremely useful tool for vampires, especially in the daytime.

"What can I do for you, Colonel?"

Ryker almost saluted before he remembered not to.

Luke smiled at his old friend. Years in the military made the habit hard to break. Ryker was a good man.

"I want you on the council. Are you interested?" Luke asked.

"Yes, sir. When do I swear in?" Ryker answered.

Andrei and Javier both grinned. Fox laughed.

"You don't even know what that means. How can you decide so fast?" Luke asked.

Ryker answered as if he'd just received orders to join the council. Ryker grinned.

"Same reason I always volunteered for every mission you led. You were the man to follow. If you thought it out, the plan was sound. I'm your man, Colonel. Always have been, always will be."

Luke sat down in the chair a bit heavily. Ryker's admission stunned him. It was genuine. Ryker had volunteered for all those missions. Luke hadn't realized the true effect he had on other men until that moment.

He'd known his alpha-male aura worked to convince weaker men of the right course of action, but he'd never realized the level of respect and faith in his ability to lead, which he inspired in stronger men.

Luke looked at the faces of the other men in the room. They stared back at him, all nodding in agreement with the sentiment behind Ryker's words.

Was Eli right? Was all of it truly based on himself? It was a sobering idea.

Luke shook his head. There had to be another angle. He refused to believe he alone was the central figure responsible for Draoithe. Absolute power corrupts absolutely, right? Council.

"Talk to Lily first. She'd have to be in on it. The new magic you'll need to learn to wield requires her agreement. You would need to take her as your queen. Give me the decision by Wednesday. We'll swear oaths on Saturday if she agrees. Get back to work. We have more vehicles on the way. Don't forget to do the Jeeps, too. Not the mustang, though. She stays original. Eli's partial to it."

Ryker clasped forearms with Luke, nodded at everybody, and teleported out of the library. Luke was about to speak when a woman screamed from down the hall.

"Griz must be awake. Shall we meet him, gentlemen?"

The Inner Circle and Andrei moved out of the library room and down the hall to Isabell's and Javier's room, loaned to Griz to recuperate. When the men arrived, Nadine, Isabell, and Artie were already there.

"What's going on?" Luke asked.

Every eye went to him.

Melody cowered away from them all. Griz looked Luke in the eye. He didn't shy away from what he didn't know. He met it head-on. The man was a grizzly bear shifter.

"Honestly, that's what I'd like to know."

The big bear of a man spoke with an even deeper baritone rumble than Kallik did. His alpha status was without question. The magic floating around him was strong. Melody nodded, her agreement still shrinking away from Luke toward Griz.

Fox nodded at Artie, and they both moved towards Melody. Luke looked at everyone else and they all left the room. Luke would handle the interview and report back later.

One-on-one would tone down the confrontation. No one wanted a fight with a hurt, angry bear who felt boxed in. Luke leaned against the doorframe, waiting.

Artie spoke to Melody first.

"Melody, dear, did you know you sleepwalk?"

Melody nodded. She was aware, good. That would make it easier to explain.

"Well, you wandered in here after we brought Griz in to rest and recuperate. We left you since you both needed to sleep. Are you alright?"

Luke looked at Griz, and Fox assessed Melody, who nodded.

Griz hadn't harmed her. Waking up to find Griz sleeping next to her startled Melody. Waking up next to a bear would be vexing, even for a big man. Melody was rather small and more of a submissive.

Artie looked at Fox, then at Luke, who nodded. Artie and Fox moved to usher Melody out of the room, and Griz rumbled low.

Luke raised an eyebrow at the convalescing bear. Griz's bear wanted his mate to stay. The animals inside the shifters in the room all knew that.

Melody froze in mid-step. Luke could see her owl knew exactly what Griz's bear wanted. She should stay with him. Melody looked confused.

Griz sighed and waved the three out of the room. Fox and Artie wasted no time leaving Luke alone with the big grouchy grizzly bear, and Luke wasn't so keen on staying, either.

Chapter Two

It Was Gone

G^{riz}

"Pardon me, but who are you, and where am I?"

The situation perplexed Griz. He wasn't well. It was difficult to maintain control over his temper, and he suffered from both pain and starvation.

Anger came easily and lingered. The woman, Melody, teased his senses, strangely messing with his concentration.

"I'm Luke Mendez, and you at Draoithe. It's a few minutes' drive outside of Tyler, TX. Do you remember what happened to you?"

"Not exactly."

Griz cocked his head to the side, thinking hard. He experienced disjointed and fuzzy memories. Things didn't fit together properly in his mind.

"I was in a warehouse. I don't know how I got there. Drugs. It had to be some kind of drug. The people were evil. The last memory I have from before it was of my favorite bar in Boulder, Colorado."

Griz turned his face away from Luke and whispered the next part. He was angry at himself for his inability to free himself and help the women. He wasn't the type of man who could stand by while someone beat a woman. His size alone gave most men pause, but his size hadn't helped him.

"I couldn't stop them. The ones in the warehouse weren't real men. What they did to those women..."

He rumbled again, and Luke growled. Griz realized he looked at a powerful shifter male who shared his feelings about how men should treat women. He felt better knowing it.

He was too weak to view Luke through the dream. Maybe the man had some kind of human decency and honor. Griz had been around too much human filth lately.

"Thanks to whoever among you splinted my broken ankle. That will take some time to heal."

He didn't know what to do about the rest. There was something wrong with his magic. Griz was too weak to focus on it. Frustrated at his current condition, he wondered again about the little woman who'd been sleeping in his arms.

"Isabell and Nadine did it after we brought you here. I'll pass on the sentiment."

Griz would have to find the two ladies and thank them.

"What happened to the women in the warehouse if I'm here?" Griz asked.

He had to know. He prayed they got out. If they'd not gotten out, he would go back after them.

He didn't know what Luke's angle was, but his reaction to the abuse of women left Griz hopeful that something had altered the women's situation as well.

"We got all seven of them out. The dragons have them in their care at the moment. No further harm will come to them. They have sanctuary here as long as they wish to stay. I wanted to extend sanctuary to you as well. Will you accept it?"

Luke offered the information readily.

What was a dragon? Some other shifter, perhaps. Griz added that to the growing list of questions he had for later.

Griz nodded yes. It aggravated him. He could accept sanctuary, but losing his independence irritated him. Trapped indoors for weeks, everything rubbed his bear the wrong way. He huffed angrily.

Could he heal his broken magic? She was there. He wasn't worthy of her, not in his current state. He gazed at the bed where she had lain next to him and closed his eyes. When Luke spoke again, he looked back at him. He seemed to want to help Griz.

"Melody's your mate, isn't she?"

"Yes, but I don't know if she'll even want me. They did things to me. Something about an antidote to cure me. I wasn't ill! I was born a bear, and I didn't want to be cured! How did they know what I was?!"

The rumble was hard to stop as his anger seemed unable to abate.

"I just wanted to find my mate. I don't seem to have total control over my magic in the waking world. In the dream, everything still works, but here, my bear is always too close to the surface. I feel angry and frustrated. Somehow, the magic no longer follows my commands. I can't shift."

Morose about the situation, there was no question who Melody was, how Griz felt about her, or what he wanted with her. Would she want a broken man?

Luke frowned. Did he understand? Griz had been a bear for over seventy-five years. He'd been born a bear shifter. He didn't know how to not be one.

Griz had to figure out how to correct what happened to him because he was unworthy of a mate in his current condition.

"There's a white witch here; the arctic fox you met in the dream? Perhaps when Artie is stronger, she can return the favor and help you. I'll discuss the situation with Fox. He may know something which could help. We need you physically healthy first, though. You need to eat and rest. Are you up for a bath?" Luke asked.

"Yes, a shower sounds good. I seem minus attire as well."

Griz wasn't in the habit of accepting help from others or asking for favors. Griz lamented his dependence on others.

His present lack of cleanliness disturbed him. He needed clothes to leave. How long had he been gone?

"Kallik is close to your size. He's already loaned some clothes to you. You don't normally rely on others for help, but I promise, you aren't a burden. You helped Artie. Draoithe values its people highly. We owe you. Besides, we built Draoithe to assist immortals who needed help. Allow us to help you," Luke requested.

"As long as I'm not a burden to you, maybe until I can walk, at least. I need help."

Griz frowned. He was one hundred and twelve years old. How had his life sank into such a low state? Who the hell would do that to a man? He had a score to settle.

If he could, he'd have a reckoning with those men from the warehouse. Whoever managed that warehouse deserved what came to them when he found them.

"Let me get Javier, and we'll help you."

Luke left the room.

Griz lumbered himself into a sitting position. He saw a large man's robe draped over the footboard of the bed. He snatched it and put it on.

Naked beneath the sheet, his state of undress didn't bother him of itself, but there were women. His mother raised him better. He wouldn't disrespect her memory.

He saw a stack of clothes and new packages of men's boxers, undershirts, and socks on the dresser. There was a shaving kit filled with a razor, shaving cream, toothbrush, shampoo, soap, etc...

Griz smiled. It seemed he'd somehow wound up in a luxury hotel at someone's home.

Things could be worse. At least he could get clean. Maybe some of his agitations would dissipate once he washed away the grime. Maybe clean and properly dressed, he could present himself to Melody and apologize.

Griz worked as a ranch hand in Colorado. He mended fences, herded cattle, tended crops, and rode in a saddle for half his life. He loved the outdoors. Farming the land, and handling horses, sheep, and cattle was good honest work.

Being weak was an unacceptable situation.

He'd relied on his strength for his entire life. His mother had reminded him to guard his strength, to always use it, and never allow it to abuse another.

It was gone.

CHAPTER THREE

Dragons?

G^{riz}

What had they done to him? He just couldn't remember, and that angered him.

How could he repair himself when he couldn't even identify the cause of the problem? He rumbled his irritation again.

Griz had never been quick to anger before. He would think it out first. In his anger and frustration, he'd even rumbled at Melody when she was the last person he ever should have. His head ached.

Maybe after he showered and ate something, he would feel better. He couldn't imagine feeling much worse.

At least he was comfortable for the moment. No one tortured him. He would build on that.

Luke came back and introduced another man, Javier. Both men were strong alphas. Griz wanted to view them through the dream, but the effort proved too taxing.

Luke was obviously in the lead. Javier was magically more powerful. Griz could feel it in the air between them.

"Griz, nice to see you awake. I hear you met Melody," Javier said.

He and Luke stepped to either side of him and hoisted him up, and waited for Griz to gain balance.

People seemed to know who he was. Had the dreamwalkers explained what had happened?

"How is she here? How did she wind up in bed with me?" Griz asked.

Not that he could complain about sleeping next to a beautiful woman. It was just rather odd and not at all how he pictured meeting her would be.

"She showed up on Thursday evening after a couple of Fox's friends sent her. She sought help. You dream talked to her off and on for days. She feared both you and for you. I gave her sanctuary until we could figure out what happened. She sleepwalks, and you were the biggest, warmest, cuddliest teddy bear she could find to curl up next to."

Luke said the last with amused sarcasm. Griz was anything but cuddly at the moment.

Griz was angry about Melody fearing him. He wouldn't have his mate fear him. That was all kinds of wrong.

He appreciated Luke's generosity more for Melody's sake than for his own. How maddening it must've been for Melody to hear the ravings of a tormented bear. He hoped he hadn't made a complete fool of himself to Melody.

He probably had a lot of explaining to do. First, he had to figure out what it was he needed to explain.

"Saturday, after you arrived, we had left the door open in case you needed attention. You were both exhausted, so we figured sleep wasn't a bad idea. She seemed more comfortable, and you seemed to relax. Win, win."

Javier explained further.

13

"I helped Kallik in the dream. Artie's dream was wrong. I had to leave because Melody called me. I went to her, but something goes wrong whenever I get close to her. It's strange. I feel lost. Time no longer works. I would just watch her in the dream."

Griz shook his head.

Something was wrong with him. It had happened when he woke to find her there in his arms, too. He just got lost in her hair and her scent of *gardenia*.

Nothing had ever felt so right, nor soothed his soul as she did. Was how he felt about her part of the problem he had controlling his anger and his bear? Was he losing his mind?

"That's not you; it's her. She's a bird. You get lost in her because she's your mate. It happens to Andrei and me all the time. Don't stop. It feels good to her, too."

Javier grinned.

"How did you know I think it feels good?"

Griz stopped moving down the hallway and narrowed suspicious eyes on Javier. Had the man spied on him earlier? Was he somehow reading his mind?

"Whoa, relax. Isabell's a phoenix. I'm her mate, and I get lost in her. I lose track of time. Nadine, Andrei's mate, is a Philippine eagle. She thinks it's like what happens when birds of prey mesmerize their prey to fly away with it, but it only works on their mates. It's a bird shifter thing. A man who loves a bird is lucky, if you ask me." Javier said.

Griz huffed, unable to argue with Javier's strange logic.

When they got to the hall bathroom, Luke turned on the shower. Luke and Javier both helped the battered Griz remove the splint so he could bathe. Luke set the shaving kit on the sink.

"We'll come back for you in twenty minutes and help you out. Are you okay with it from here?" Javier asked.

"Yeah, thanks, guys. I think I can handle things."

Griz nodded. The shower called to him.

"If you need immediate help before we get back, clap your hands twice, and a servant assigned to your care will respond immediately," Luke said.

He followed Javier out of the expansive bathroom.

Servant? The people were over the top. He preferred to do things for himself. Griz shook his head and hopped, one footed, into the shower.

The bathroom was nice. It had both a jetted tub and a shower, but only one sink. The shower was easier to manage. Griz slid the door closed behind him.

Griz washed his hair twice. He debated washing it three times, but decided against it. It took him nearly fifteen minutes to scrub the filth from his skin. The damn warehouse stench finally went away. Then he toweled off and hop stepped to the sink to brush his teeth and shave his almost full beard stubble.

He dropped the razor on the floor accidentally just before finishing his shave. He slapped the sink top twice in frustration and searched in the shaving kit for another razor. With his ankle messed up, he couldn't easily retrieve the fallen razor.

The bathroom door flew open, and a man wearing robes asked if he required help. It was the bastard from the warehouse. Griz roared at the man and tried to swipe at him with a clawed paw.

The robed figure stepped back, puzzled. Griz's paw was still a hand. That frustrated Griz further. Javier appeared behind the servant.

"What the hell is that bastard doing here?" Griz rumbled.

He had a lot of anger inside, and he wanted the man from the warehouse dead. If he could get to the evil bastard, Griz would end him.

Why did his shift not work? That doubly pissed him off.

"Strip!"

Javier ordered the man from the warehouse as he picked up the fallen razor and handed it back to Griz.

The man immediately disrobed in front of them. Griz hopped back against the sink, away from what he saw.

"Redress and leave. Bring Griz clothing."

Javier ordered the man away.

"What the hell was that?" Griz asked.

His anger slowly faded as his shock overrode it. The servant had none of his masculine parts. Someone had cut or burned away his masculine parts.

Served the bastard right for what he'd done to those women, but it unsettled Griz. Maybe death the servant didn't require death after all.

"He's no longer a man. He's a dragonsworn servant for Draoithe. The dragons found him guilty of failing to follow the Ri ruirech's laws. They sentenced him to service. For the crime of failing to act like a man, he lost his manhood. He won't fail to show proper respect again. His fate is worse than death. He serves eternally. Order him as you will," Javier said.

"Dragons?"

CHAPTER FOUR

Hopeful Smile

G*riz*

Luke had mentioned them before. Who or what were dragons? Griz finished shaving as Javier spoke. He needed to feel clean as much as he needed information.

"The dragons are protectors of the realm. They serve the Ri ruirech and the Ruiri of Draoithe. They protect the people of the Druid pack and any under the Ri ruirech's protection. Luke is the Ri ruirech of Draoithe and the alpha male of the Druid pack at Draoithe. He offered you sanctuary. No harm will come to you. If the servant displeases you, tell the servant. He will confess to the dragons on Friday at sunset, and they'll punish him. I think the dragons hope one or more will need punishment," Javier explained.

"This place is strange."

Griz remained a little confused.

Javier laughed.

"It grows on you."

Griz had accepted Luke's offer of sanctuary. He might need more time to puzzle that shit out. He placed his toothbrush and razor in the shaving kit, along with the toothpaste and the shampoo.

Dragons? Where the hell did dragons come from? They were in the warehouse. They worked for Luke.

The servant returned with Griz's underclothes, black jeans, and a dress shirt. Griz snatched the things away from the servant.

"Don't look at me. I don't like the feel of your eyes on me," Griz rumbled.

The dragonsworn lowered his head immediately. Javier just grinned.

"Will the master require anything else?" the servant asked.

"Shoes, size twelve. Boots would be nice, but tennis shoes will do," Griz said.

"I'm not permitted to leave the grounds, Master. I don't know if Draoithe has the items on hand. Is time a factor?" the servant asked.

"No, and neither is money," Javier interrupted.

"Speak with the other men and learn all their shoe sizes. Then do the same for all the women. List it all and present the list along with Griz's request to Artie while in the presence of Fox. She'll see to it."

The dragonsworn bowed and hurried off to begin his work. The fool had positively beamed at the task assigned to him. It was creepy. Javier was right. Forcing the men from the warehouse into eternal service was a good punishment for their crimes.

They wouldn't be abusing any more women. The way the dragons accomplished that made Griz uncomfortable, but a man who couldn't respect women never deserved a chance to be with one. That fool sure as hell would never hurt another one again.

Griz thought it out and decided he approved of the dragonsworn, even if he didn't particularly like them. He still didn't want any of them looking at him or hanging out near him for long. They made him angry, along with just about everything else.

"Shall we get some food for you?"

Luke asked from the doorway.

"We saved you a plate. Do you like lasagna?"

Griz nodded. All the food sounded good at the moment. He hoped they had bear-sized portions. He felt like eating enough to hibernate.

"Fox likes to play with his food, just say nothing. He's touchy about it, but he's an excellent chef."

Javier grinned as Griz used the two men as crutches to move down the hall to the dining room.

They made their way to the dining room to find Eli and Isabell drinking tea with Melody. Griz settled into a chair. Luke went to serve himself tea and coffee for Javier. Javier took a pan of lasagna out of the oven, looked at Griz, cut it in half, then set it on a plate.

He added garlic breadsticks and served a large salad in a separate bowl. Luke brought Griz a glass of iced tea and left the pitcher on the table. Javier handed the overloaded plate to the bear and set the salad down with a napkin and silverware.

They understood bear-sized portions! Shifters needed to eat a lot because their magic rapidly burned calories.

Griz hadn't eaten well in a couple of weeks. He needed food in the worst way. Lots of it as fast as possible sounded good.

"We need to figure out sleeping arrangements."

Luke seemed grumpy about the subject. Eli smiled at him.

"Why don't you stop worrying about stuff I've already taken care of?"

Luke relaxed next to her. Eli seemed to have the magic touch with Luke.

"Ryker and Lily moved to Mihaela's old room so he can get more work done. Mihaela moved in with Kallik. Melody has agreed to give her bed here to Griz so Isabell and Javier can have their space back."

Eli explained the arrangements.

"Where does Melody sleep?" Luke asked.

"She doesn't have to give up her bed for me. I won't accept that."

Griz rumbled. He was upset his condition might cause his snowy owl to be mistreated. Melody moved to the chair next to Griz's and sat close to him. Griz looked at her.

She smiled shyly at him. She answered the warning in the rumble, just as she had frozen when he hadn't wanted her to leave earlier.

He understood she was a submissive. His snowbird needed him to be her alpha.

"Okay, we'll share it then?" Melody whispered.

She gave him what his bear wanted. He looked into her golden eyes, nodded, and fell into her.

She was so beautiful. He wanted to touch her face and feel her hair. He wanted the scent of *gardenia* to wrap him around.

From far away, he heard Javier say something to Melody about sending Griz back. That man interfered. He need not speak to Melody. Griz rumbled low and dangerously at Javier without taking his eyes off Melody.

"Griz, will you not eat?" Melody asked.

He looked at the plate in front of him, and the spell broke. Griz shook his head, picked up his fork, and ate; not because it smelled good, or out of hunger, but mostly because Melody wanted him to eat.

"See, I told you. Be careful with that, Melody. Nadine fell asleep and trapped Andrei for nearly eleven hours on a sofa once without realizing it. He wasn't upset, but it can be disorienting," Isabell said.

"I see what you mean. Then is it true? Griz is my mate?" Melody asked.

Griz looked up to see Isabell nodding, and Melody smiled up at him shyly. She knew. She didn't seem upset.

Griz felt hopeful for the first time since he'd learned that he'd inadvertently tormented her with a dreamtalk while they tortured him.

"You were always in my barn, and you even smell like *baled hay in the sun*. You came to see me, didn't you?"

Griz smiled and nodded. He'd visited her dream often the week before someone took him captive.

"How did you find me there?" Melody asked.

"I asked the dream to show my mate. It always took me to your barn in your dream. Sometimes, you were there, other times you were far away, but I knew you built the dream and would return. I'm not skilled enough to build a dream to which I can call another, but waiting for you in yours let me see into your life. I wanted to know you."

Griz spoke softly to her.

"You called me into your dream, Griz. I saw you in an awful place. You talked to me. Do you remember?"

She seemed confused, shaking her head. Griz looked at her.

He didn't know her then. Was that even possible?

Wait, he knew her. She was Melody Brooks. She'd spoken with him in the dream. The memory made him smile.

"You're Melody Brooks. We spoke in the dream. I asked you to seek help. I remember now."

She gave him a part of his missing memory.

He ate some more lasagna as he thought about Melody Brooks. She eased his frustration. The anger seemed less pressing.

"And you're Enyeto Locklear, but you prefer to be called Griz. I did what you asked. I found help."

Melody had a hopeful smile.

CHAPTER FIVE

The Conversation

Griz

Melody was young, his snowbird. She needed validation from him. She was a submissive.

She'd done the best possible job. Melody had found a group of immortals who saved not only himself, but seven others as well. The people not only saved them and gave them sanctuary so they could rest and heal, but they punished the ones responsible.

"You found the best help possible, snowbird. Thank you. I might not have made it if you hadn't gotten help."

Griz admitted the truth to her. He'd lasted a long time for a shifter without his mate. He'd almost lost hope of finding her. She'd saved him twice.

"No, I could never allow that. I... I need you. I just didn't know what to do," she whispered.

Griz looked at her small little face. She needed him, and he needed her desperately. He didn't know what was wrong with him, but she'd given him back a small piece.

She'd been with him in the dream. Melody knew what he'd lost. He needed to know what they did to him. He hoped she would help him.

"I need you, too, but I'm broken. Will you wait for me? I would be worthy of you first," Griz said.

"I'll wait, but you're already worthy."

She smiled at him.

Griz finished the plate and looked at the oven as he ate the last of the breadsticks. Luke noticed and jumped up. He took the pan of lasagna out of the oven and asked Griz if he wanted more. Griz nodded.

"Can you finish it?"

Griz nodded again.

He'd felt as if his stomach digested itself earlier. Griz could finish it. He only hoped no one started calling him Garfield.

He was hungry. Luke smiled and nodded as he turned the rest of the lasagna out of the pan onto Griz's plate. Luke left the pan to soak in the sink.

Griz ate quickly. When the plate cleared again, Griz felt a little better. He finished the rest of the salad and another basket of breadsticks, as well.

Luke spoke to Melody.

"I hope you've decided Draoithe will host you longer than the weekend?"

Melody looked up at Luke and then back at Griz.

"I would like to stay. Please, if you'll allow me some time to seek employment, I'll pay for my stay. I know you can't stay anywhere for free."

Griz wanted to tell Luke he'd pay for Melody when Luke spoke again.

"Nonsense, sanctuary guests stay for free. If it makes you feel better, I might know of something that would help Draoithe. You had a degree in fashion design. I may have a job for you. If you'd be interested?"

Luke waited for her to process what he said. Was he offering Melody a permanent job?

"What kind of job?"

Melody asked with genuine interest, echoing Griz's thoughts.

"We need a tailor on staff. Draoithe will have a lot of formal and semi-formal functions, plus everyone needs business clothes and other things of that nature. We're building a retreat. The hospitality industry requires all the employees to look the part. Would you be interested in designing and creating uniforms, business, and formal clothes with and without Draoithe logos for all levels of employees at Draoithe? You could even open a boutique and sell clothing items to the guests at high-end prices."

Luke made her an offer she couldn't refuse.

"I would like to market my ideas? It would take a staff of people to help me. I still haven't met everyone here, but Eli and Isabell told me there are twenty-eight people and nineteen servants in residence. That's a lot of clothes. Do you even have a sewing machine?" Melody asked.

"See, that's why we need you. I don't know how any of that works. I just know I need clothes and so do all my people. You would never run out of work. The retreat won't be operational until the end of July next year. You'd have about a year to get your first designs approved and sent out to seamstresses and tailors to be made to fit everyone. I'll even give you a salary, cell phone, and transportation along with room and board. You'd have a budget, and Draoithe will supply whatever startup and continuing equipment you'd need, including the workspace and the boutique. Will you join us?"

Luke sweetened the deal.

"What would I need to do? If I said 'yes'? I mean, how do I join?"

Melody was curious.

Griz could see she wanted what Luke offered, but she feared it. If she joined the pack, more powerful people could use her submissive nature against her. If she'd studied, it would be cruel to deny her the opportunity.

He would have to stay to win her and protect her from the alphas who might unknowingly overwork her. Griz didn't know about that. His life in Colorado had felt good. He longed to return to working the land and being outdoors.

"Petition the council at lunch next Sunday. They'll review your application, and if they approve it, I'll let you know Tuesday or Wednesday. Put in the order with Artie for startup equipment and submit to Eli and me the following Saturday as your alpha leaders. You would become part of the Druid pack at Draoithe, and you could begin work the following Monday. You make your hours. Run your show. What do you say? Will you stay and learn about us this week, ask questions, and let us know something by next Sunday?"

Luke remained hopeful she'd at least consider staying to learn about Draoithe.

Griz felt as if Luke truly wanted the snowy owl to stay. Griz needed to learn what the place was all about, too.

Like what was a Ri ruirech and a Ruiri? Where did those dragons Javier had spoken of fit into all of it? And the money confused him.

The people acted as if money wasn't a problem. Luke and Javier had served him dinner and claimed that Fox had cooked it. They had servants. None of it made sense. Griz had some funds, but he was nowhere near independently wealthy.

Luke wanted Melody to not only work for Draoithe but also join the Druid pack. She wasn't a canine shifter. She was a bird. Why would he want her to join the pack as well?

He realized Melody looked at him to get his reaction before she answered. She'd already deferred to his alpha status in their brand-new relationship.

He couldn't say 'no' to her. It wasn't his place to tell her what to do, but she wanted his approval. He smiled at her.

"Luke, I'd like to learn, too. Would it be possible for me to make a petition to join you as well?"

Griz gave Melody the answer she needed without telling her what to do. She smiled back at him. She wanted what Luke offered. Her snowy owl wanted her mate. If Griz stayed, she could have both.

"You could. What do you do? What skills would you bring to the table if we were to consider you as well?" Luke asked.

"In Colorado, I was a rancher. I worked the fields at harvest time and planting season; I tended to flocks of both sheep and cattle and did general farm labor, mending fences, breaking horses, feeding livestock, cleaning barns, baling hay..." Griz said.

He smiled as he spoke about his work. He loved the outdoors. His work had always used his strength and had fulfilled him. If Griz could work again, he'd be happy. He could even consider leaving Colorado. Was there a place for a man like him?

"Have you ever stocked a pond or lake with fish?" Javier asked.

He'd been silent but grew interested in the conversation when Griz spoke about outdoor work.

CHAPTER SIX

Boots

G *riz*

"No, but it sounds like fun. I'd be willing to try it."

Griz grinned. Fish sounded good. He could seriously eat some fish.

"We have this Kodiak bear who keeps eating the fish in the larger lake. I'm worried it won't be good for fishing for retreat guests, so I thought about stocking the smaller lake just for fishing expeditions. I'd need some help with that."

Javier mused out loud.

"When did we decide there would be fishing expeditions?" Luke asked.

"We haven't yet, but I like to fish. Kallik likes to eat fish. There's a bit of an issue. It would be a nice outdoor package if we added it to the horseback riding trails. We need to build some canoes and a dock on the larger lake as well, and probably a small stable at the smaller lake. I mean, it's some acres from the retreat house. We can't all teleport or fly on the ground as Andrei can."

Javier suggested some more things which needed to be done at Draoithe. It was a startup. Griz wondered what 'flying on the ground' meant.

"I can help with all of that. There'll be horses? I love horses. I would help you maintain all your stables, and I can shoe horses as well," Griz said.

He grew seriously interested in all the outdoor work.

"You farmed, too?"

Eli asked, suddenly interested in him.

"Yes ma'am. We mostly grew alfalfa for hay and corn for feed, but I reckon driving a tractor to farm something else would be about the same," Griz said.

"No tractors. We chose horses over four-wheelers to keep the land as natural as possible. I want all organic, horse, and plow. Vegetables for the restaurant and beef cattle might be good. More cost-effective. Draw less outside interest. What do you know about barn raising? Can I run cattle on forested land?"

Luke was curious.

"I can raise a barn if I have help, and I would need to see the land to tell you about the cattle. We would need draft horses to till Amish style. If you want to go off-grid, I can help you with that, too. Rain barrels and gutters, purple pipes, solar panels, and batteries all make a place more self-sufficient. We did all of it in Colorado. The ranch received good prices on beef cattle, too."

"We tried dairy cattle, but it wasn't profitable. I think if you did it on a small scale, not to sell but to use, it might make it better. You would need to keep livestock away from predators and immortals to avoid accidental loss. I think if you had enough land, you could farm it easily. Can we tour the land?" Griz asked.

Griz found himself a bit excited about the potential project. A small scale nearly autonomous ranch supporting a retreat intrigued him. He considered how it might operate.

If there were enough people to help, the dairy side might be good to make cheese and butter for the restaurant. He'd always wanted to try beekeeping as well. He was a bear, after all. Raw honey sounded good.

"I think maybe you should heal first," Javier said, chuckling.

"Sorry, I got excited about being outdoors. I hate being inside for too long. Feels like I haven't seen the sky in forever."

Griz lamented his current circumstances.

Melody touched his hand, and Griz brightened. Being indoors at the moment wasn't all bad. At least he had a beautiful snowy owl to pay attention to.

"I know what you mean. The pack runs every Saturday night. It's required of those in residence and able-bodied. It ensures everyone gets together and enjoys the natural world at least once a week, no matter how busy they get during the week. Shifters get to be in their animal form, and birds fly. Even vampires like the social aspect."

Luke filled in some details for Griz and Melody.

Vampires were real? Draoithe was strange.

Griz saw Melody's eyes light up at the mention of flying. Griz didn't like heights, but Melody was an owl. Night flying would be something she enjoyed. He would like to see that.

"How about we get you a couple of pairs of hiking boots and as soon as you're well, we'll take a trip out to the land. You can have a grand tour. It might be Tuesday or Wednesday afternoon. Maybe you can help me figure out where to put a barn, a boutique, and a garden. Oh, we already have chickens and rabbits, too."

Luke looked at Griz, then Melody, then back to Griz. Griz grinned at the mention of the small livestock.

Melody would do what Griz wanted. Luke knew it. She was a true submissive, and she'd already decided Griz was her alpha.

29

However, she was an owl, and keeping a wild bird in a cage is not appropriate. Griz didn't want her to feel trapped or forced to do what he wanted. Griz looked at Melody.

"Would you go with me to see the retreat, Snowbird?" Griz asked.

"Yes, I'd like to see it. A boutique sounds interesting," Melody said.

"Can I tag along? I can draw up the plans to send to the designer. I would love to draw Melody's vision for a boutique. We should probably get a theme and build a small bistro/coffee shop, so immortals could have a public space to gather in the early morning, as well. It wouldn't compete with Lily's restaurant. We could sell clothing and grab a tea or coffee or a bagel or breakfast sandwich. We can add it in phase three with Javier's day spa and build it all close to Labyrinth Art."

Isabell got excited. Javier nodded. Eli smiled.

"We don't have anyone to operate all these businesses, and we haven't got to phase three yet," Luke complained.

"We need to find out if any of the ladies the dragons care for would be interested in helping us. They might be just what we need."

Eli sounded hopeful. Luke shook his head.

"Fine, they're good ideas. We'll leave them on the table and shelve anything unfeasible when we get to phase three. I think we're getting ahead of ourselves. Maybe we should get moved in first and see what's next. A morning coffee shop sounds good, though."

Luke shared his reservations, but he liked the ideas floating around the table.

"It's late. Let's go so these guys can get some rest."

Eli stood up.

"Hold on. There's something I gotta get from the library first," Luke said.

He disappeared down the hall.

Javier came around to help steady Griz as he rose from the table, too. Javier clapped his hands twice. A servant in robes appeared.

"Move all of Griz's things to Melody's room," Javier said.

Luke returned with a cane, which he offered to Griz with a smile.

"Here, I thought this might help you get some of your independence back. It's lucky. It helped me win a tiger once."

Griz smiled and thanked Luke as he accepted the cane. He used it to make his way slowly down the hall to Melody's room.

He saw her battered suitcase in the corner. She had flown from California just to help him. She'd saved him.

The clothes Kallik had loaned him, the shaving kit, and the new packages of men's undergarments were on top of the chest of drawers in the corner. Men's tennis shoes and a pair of boots sat next to the chest. Griz smiled at the boots.

CHAPTER SEVEN

From Experience

*M*elody

They were alone in the room. Melody was nervous. Griz looked bigger standing up than he'd appeared sitting in the dining room. He was taller than Luke and physically more imposing. He had dark brown hair and dark brown eyes.

Why had she decided it was a good idea to share her space with him? She knew he was her mate. Her owl wanted him close. Only, he was... enormous.

She breathed in his scent of *baled hay in the sun,* and she calmed a little. He smelled like her barn in her dream. How was that possible?

Griz tried to make her comfortable. He moved slowly and deliberately toward the boots.

She watched him move. He was a bear of a man. Yet he wasn't clumsy, nor was he brutish. His mind was sharp, and his movements precise.

Melody had discussed her sleepwalking with Artie, Eli, and Isabell. They'd answered her questions. Artie grew tired, and Fox had led her away to sleep. Isabell had stayed with her and Eli and offered her bird shifter knowledge.

Everything Isabell had said had been true, especially the part about how she could practically mesmerize the big giant bear as easily as a field mouse. She didn't even need to try. He just seemed to fall into her.

That felt good. It lessened her fear knowing he was her lifemate. Finding him so soon in her shifter life meant she didn't need to worry about fading.

She liked the man as much as she'd liked the bear in her barn in her dream. He leaned down and picked up the boots, careful not to put pressure on his broken ankle.

He sat down in a chair and leaned the cane against the armrest. He pulled a card out of the boots. Melody was curious about it.

"What does it say?"

She sat on the edge of the bed, nervous.

"*Griz, I heard you needed these. I wanted to say thanks again for helping Eli and me in the dream. Your expertise was invaluable. The shoes are new. They say size twelve and a half, but were a bit too tight for me. Until you can buy your own, perhaps these will help. If you feel up to it, there's a maned wolf from the warehouse turned without consent who needs help. We're going to attempt a healing Monday evening. If you would like to dreamwalk, I'd appreciate the help. Thanks, Kallik.*"

Griz read the card aloud.

Melody liked his deep, rumbly baritone voice. Everything about the man spoke to her. He felt like strength, and he was powerful.

Griz felt good to her. She wanted to be near him. Her owl responded instantly to his bear. He made her feel safe. He would take care of her.

For the last year, since learning she was an owl shifter, her life had gone off track. She had her degree from college, but she hadn't been able to find work in her field.

She'd spent most of her savings trying to make ends meet in California and had overextended herself when Griz started dream talking to her. Her employer fired her because she didn't show up for work that week.

It hadn't taken Luke long to convince her to stay at Draoithe for the weekend. She had little to return to. Luke had even offered her an awesome job opportunity.

If Griz left Draoithe, she would go with him. Her owl wanted to be near him. Getting another job opportunity, as well as the one Luke handed her, would never happen. Would he stay?

Melody smiled at the kind words on the card. Everyone at Draoithe seemed nice and down to earth. The new servants were creepy, but otherwise, it seemed like a good place for a shifter to be.

Would Griz consider living at Draoithe, or had he only asked because he didn't want to hurt her feelings? Did he even want her as a lifemate? What if he was happy with his life as it was?

"Do they fit?"

Griz tried one boot on his good foot.

He grinned at her, happy with the boots.

"Yeah, and I even like the style. I wonder what Kallik does here."

"I think Isabell told said he was the stable master. I haven't met him yet. He wasn't here when I arrived."

Melody answered his query with what knowledge she had gained.

"Draoithe has stables?"

Griz grinned at that thought.

Melody liked his grin. It was genuine and made his strong-jawed face seem less imposing.

When he wasn't smiling, he was handsome, but it was in a hard form. Another wouldn't easily mislead or take advantage of him.

34

When he smiled, his easy-going nature showed through. She didn't think he smiled often.

Melody nodded.

"They're under construction, and Javier has been feeding the two colts every day. Fox told him Friday morning he would do it Saturday if they didn't get back in time."

"They've barely begun building out their stables then. I would like to work with Kallik, I think. If Luke's plans are what I think, this would be a great opportunity. I wouldn't have to give it up in a few years."

Griz shared his thoughts with her.

He confused Melody. She was happy that he seemed to want to talk to her, but why would he give up his work?

"Give it up? Why would you do that?" she asked.

Griz stared at her. Melody shrank back a bit. Had she asked something wrong?

"How old are you?"

Griz asked instead of answering her.

"Tw… twenty-six," Melody stammered.

Did her age matter? How old was he? He looked to be in his early thirties, maybe thirty-five. Then she remembered shifters lived forever.

Eli had tried to explain immortality. There was too much information at once. She couldn't keep up.

"Oh, well, that explains everything."

Was that good or bad? Was he upset she was twenty-six? She couldn't change that. She frowned.

What if he didn't find her attractive or thought of her as a child because of her age? She was young. She wasn't dumb, just inexperienced with the magic in the immortal realm.

"How old are you?" she asked.

If he knew her age, it was only fair she knew his age.

"I'm one hundred twelve. When you live in the human world, failure to show your age can become a problem. Many immortals drop out of sight or move every twenty-five years before people notice. They reinvent themselves."

Eli had said something about Draoithe being a place for immortals to do something like that. They could come to the retreat, take a vacation, and be themselves for a bit, then move on to the next chapter in their lives.

Griz certainly didn't look one hundred and twelve. He must've reinvented himself three or four times already if he lived among people.

Melody wasn't sure about that. Could she reinvent herself and leave all her friends behind? Luke's offer to stay looked even more inviting.

Melody didn't realize it before, but all of her friends would eventually be gone. She didn't think she could stand to lose everyone or just keep giving them up over and over.

"Yeah, I see what you're thinking. It's hard. If you stay too long anywhere, it becomes hard to walk away from the people you trust, admire, and love. Many shifters fade around a hundred. Especially if they never find their lifemate. It's hard to live for eternity alone."

Griz looked as if he spoke from experience.

CHAPTER EIGHT

Together In The Dream

M^{*elody*}

"Griz, I think I want to stay here. I'm not strong like you. I don't think I could keep reinventing myself. Luke made me the best job offer I've ever had."

Melody bit her bottom lip.

Why was she telling him all that? They barely met.

Did he care whether she wanted to stay? She thought she would go with him if he left. What if that's not what he wanted?

Nothing she'd learned from her grandmother or Isabell prepared her to deal with any of it.

"I know. I read it on your face. He wants you to stay. It's why he made the offer. Why? Why does he want to keep you?" Griz asked.

He had a point. Why would Luke offer her a job like that out of nowhere with no proof of her ability? It was too good to be true.

Even Luke had known she would question the offer and his motives. He was counting on it. He asked her to stay again and learn.

He wanted her to discover the answer. Did he think if she learned more about Draoithe, it would make her more likely to stay?

"I don't know. He wants me to find out. He thinks if I figure out what he's up to, I'll want to stay. That's why he asked me to stay for another week and learn. He's counting on me puzzling it all out."

Melody shared her thoughts with Griz.

Griz made her feel comfortable. She liked the man. He was smart.

Maybe they should team up on things and learn together. If they did, she might get to know him better and find out if she had a place with him.

"It almost feels as if he made you the offer in front of me on purpose. He gets something out of that, too. I don't know what. Nothing feels evil. Luke has ulterior motives, but they aren't harmful, whatever they are. He's a guardian type. He wants to protect his investment. That's for sure."

Griz shared his thoughts with her again.

The easy talk intrigued Melody. Their sharing was mutually respectful.

Most of the guys her age never stopped attempting to climb into bed with her. Rebuffing them had become second nature to her.

Shed tried a couple of relationships in college. Nothing serious. She had given up on them rather easily.

There had to be more than just sex in a good relationship. Sex should be good, too. It hadn't been.

She focused on what Griz said about Luke being a guardian. It fit with what she knew of him. He'd acted protective of her and everyone else ever since she arrived.

It wasn't a new thing for him. He went after more people to protect. It wasn't just the women he protected, either. He guarded his friends as well. They mattered to him.

"He wanted you to open the subject with him about you staying. If he offered me the job, he knew you'd be curious. If he'd offered it to you outright, you would've viewed his offer as a charity. Or, if he makes you work for it, you'll own it. I can see your independence streak. You prefer to be your own man in control of your destiny. You're a strong alpha male. Luke has a lot of alpha men around him. He's used to dealing with them. I'd say he prefers it that way."

Melody offered him her thoughts on the matter. Griz scowled when she discussed the alpha nature of the other men, but had said nothing. She hoped she hadn't made him angry somehow.

Melody grew silent. Griz struggled with something she'd said. Silent. she waited for him.

Finally, he looked directly at her and spoke low with tightly controlled anger.

"The bear in me doesn't like that you notice these qualities in other men. What you say is true, but the bear is possessive of you and wants your attention focused on him, not the other males."

Griz spoke as if he were trying hard to focus and maintain his control.

Melody rose and went to him. She reached out and touched his face.

At only five feet and one inch, Melody wasn't tall. Griz wasn't much shorter than she was while seated. He looked up at her.

"Griz, my owl shrinks away from all of them. She wants you. You're the only one who doesn't frighten me. I, I feel... safe... only with you. If you leave, my owl wants to go with you. I only came to Draoithe because I needed to find you. I didn't have the strength to help you on my own."

Melody admitted to him her true thoughts.

Griz fell into her. She felt him get lost in her eyes. The powerful bear wanted her.

It was heady. She liked it. Then she realized he was no longer having to fight to maintain control.

He was relaxed. The anger had left him. That felt even better. Melody enjoyed easing his emotions. He'd said he was broken.

Maybe tomorrow they could work on fixing him. For the moment, he was better.

"Griz, are you tired? I could use some rest. Will you lie down?" he nodded.

"I'm tired. What are your wishes? I may have inadvertently led you to choose this arrangement when I rumbled my displeasure at you leaving me when we woke earlier, but I don't want you to be fearful of me. I'm having difficulty remaining in control."

He spoke to her gently again, ashamed of his earlier behavior. He wanted to be a gentleman for her. She could go along with that.

"Can we share the bed as we did before I woke up and realized you weren't a dream?" Melody asked.

Griz nodded.

"I'll go get changed for bed. Do you need any help?" Melody asked.

"No. I can manage. The food helped."

Griz smiled his thanks to her.

She pulled out a pair of loose shorts and an old t-shirt from her luggage and slipped out to the bathroom to change. When she returned, Griz sat on the edge of the bed in his boxers and his undershirt.

Somehow, he looked bigger when undressed. He was still handsome, but the bruises were more visible. Melody sucked in her breath as she realized how bad his physical condition was.

She trembled. Her tears fell as she looked at the damage done to her bear. He shouldn't have been so horribly abused. Seeing him hurt made her heartache for him.

"Hey, what's wrong, Snowbird?"

Melody wrenched her eyes away from the visible ugly purple bruises on his chest and arms and looked at his deep brown eyes. His eyes didn't reveal the pain he'd suffered.

"I don't like that they hurt you. It frustrates me to know they tried to take you from me. Whoever's responsible for all of this needs to pay for the evil that's been done."

Melody whispered her anger to him.

He opened his arms to her, and she went to him. He held her close and whispered to her.

"Do not cry for me. I'm strong. I'll heal. Just help me regain myself, and if you want them to pay, we shall make it happen."

He wanted to reassure her.

He hurt, yet he held her. Melody sniffed back her tears. She had her bear.

She would help him heal, and she would keep him. No one would hurt him anymore. They were safe.

He gathered her up and turned with her, and laid her on the bed. Griz lay next to her and pulled the covers over them. He wrapped his arms around her as he had before, and she snuggled into his chest. He smelled so good, like *baled hay in the sun.*

They were both in her barn a few minutes later, in the dream. She was a snowy owl, and he was an enormous grizzly bear. She dropped to the barn floor and roosted on his paw. He snuffled at her, laying his bear's head on top of his other paw next to her, and they rested together in the dream.

CHAPTER NINE

With Menace

rtie

A Artie and Duncan had left Melody with Isabell and Eli. Artie was tired. She needed to sleep more. Kallik had been right. Food, rest, and water were her focus. She was always thirsty.

They got ready for bed. She was too tired to do anything but sleep. Duncan was solicitous of her. Something was wrong. She felt strange.

"Duncan, everything feels different. I don't feel like myself. I don't feel like I want to fade, but I'm not comfortable with myself either."

Artie tried to tell her mate what was wrong. She wasn't sure if she explained it well.

"Should I call Kallik or Eli? Do you think you're regressing? You haven't tried to use any magic, have you?" Duncan asked.

"No. The dream's still good. I think we fixed it. No. I've used no magic. I'm too tired and weak to wield the white magic, anyway. I feel less connected to you, though. It's strange."

Telepathy is nice. I enjoy thinking across the room rather than needing to touch. I can even extend my awareness of the link between us into your emotions. It's bright and vibrant. I could never do that before. Your feelings were never so clear to me. That part of our bond is so much better.

Artie frowned.

I think I miss the fealty service oath magic. It has completely changed. I can feel the constriction of it as your queen, but it's not compelling, nor is it tight to me as it once was. It's rather disconcerting.

"Will you sleep with me?"

Duncan asked her because he always asked.

She nodded shyly. After four centuries, she was still shy with him.

They lay down together, and she took comfort in her lifemate's alpha strength. He made her feel safe. She loved him unconditionally. Duncan was *everything*.

"Rest, Artie. Perhaps you just need time to adjust to the newness. If you regain your strength in a couple of weeks, and it still bothers you, we can revisit the problem. Will that work? Can you give it the two weeks Kallik wants for your recovery?"

He begged her.

"Yes, it isn't pressing. You just asked me to tell you if anything felt strange to me. I wanted you to know. The magic of the Ruiri is foreign to me as a woman. You're the only one who knows how it works. If there's something wrong, I know you can fix it."

Artie yawned.

"It would involve magic, so I would have to wait, anyway. As long as I have you, Duncan, everything else can wait."

"You're everything to me, Artie. Sleep now and recuperate. I need you, or I can't do this. I love you, my queen."

Duncan loved her. Artie knew it. His love was what she drowned every day. She could never give him up.

"I love you, too."

Artie yawned again. Sleep called her. Sleeping in Duncan's arms, smelling *ink on parchment,* and feeling Duncan's love pour into her mind made all her troubles fade away.

Luke

"Fox, you didn't see it. I'm telling you. We need them all. Look, honestly, why am I even having this argument with you? You're the keeper of the strays, for crying out loud," Luke complained.

"You saw a future in the dragon's glass. That doesn't mean it's the only future. The glass showed you one vision. Just because we have one more council ring to give away doesn't mean it should go to Griz. I'm saying you should step back."

Fox tried to reason with Luke. Luke just shook his head.

"Give me a better explanation for it all, and I'll reconsider my next move."

"He can't give you a better explanation because he doesn't have one. He's right about all of this being a bit too much of a coincidence."

Javier chimed in.

"I think Isabell's right somehow. The magic keeps balancing us. The image in the spooky mirror was exactly as Eli suggested the council should be. If we keep Melody, Griz will stay. I thought it was worth the offer," Luke said.

"I think you just like the idea of having an in-house seamstress. Maybe Eli complimented you on how good you look in tailored clothes or something."

Javier grinned. Luke scowled.

"That would be nice, but not the real reason. You backed my play last night. Why are you on Fox's side now?"

Luke demanded.

44

"I'm not. I'm playing devil's advocate. Fox knows more about magic and dragons than either of us. Hear him out, then decide," Javier said.

"Are you sure the man you saw was Griz?" Fox asked.

"No, but I'd never seen him before. The woman was Melody, and she was a hundred percent Griz's mate. He falls into that owl worse than Javier with Isabell," Luke said.

"Are you sure you want the dragons in the pack?" Fox asked.

"I think so, yes. They're shifters, after all. I want the pack big enough to be a threat to Elliot. If we're large enough, we aren't as vulnerable. I don't want Draoithe to wind up like the Cioaran Enclave. If all the dragons had a Valkyrie, then we wouldn't have the strange handler orgy you had in the past. None of the dragons seemed overly fond of it. They specifically came here to seek their life mates. I think it would work. They won't be part of the council. They were clearly on the outside of the stone circle, the same as they were at the ceremony, except for the women with them. Makes sense as they see themselves as servants to us, technically."

Luke was thinking out loud.

"So your plan... make offers to the women to join the pack and take positions at Draoithe so they will want to stay and become Valkyries?" Fox asked.

"The dragons want to be part of the pack already. They have to wait until their Valkyries join to be added. The dragons already have positions at Draoithe. I want the women to be safe and feel like they have a place. Just like what we did with Isabell. That was partly why I made the offer to Melody last night," Luke said.

"What do these dragon ladies bring to the table?" Fox asked.

"I don't know yet. Eli suggested they may offer solutions to the positions we have yet to fill. I wanted to meet with them, interview them, then make them offers. I sent an invitation to Ash first. He and Raven will be here at noon. Do you want in on it?" Luke asked.

The pack had to grow. They had to be careful, but fighting against Elliot was bigger than just a warehouse takedown. They needed a small army.

"I want in. I'm still backing your play because I think it's worth it to find out what these people could do for us. We still have to consider what we need in the phase three-building project. We added a coffee shop and a boutique last night; along with a canoe dock and a fishing venue, complete with a small stable area. Land might need to be cleared for the farm, and then we need to look into running cattle on any unused area," Javier said.

"Yeah, count me in, too. I'm curious. Only one woman was a shifter. Smoke told me Keira is a Nephilim and can see the future in the aura of others sometimes. How many interviews are you planning today?" Fox asked.

"Maybe two. I want to meet with Raven, then maybe Keira. I sent the invitation to Smoke and Keira to be here at one o'clock," Luke said.

Fox frowned.

"You know, I'm supposed to be the head of intelligence, right?"

Fox groused about being left out of the loop.

"Artie was more important, Fox. You know that. Hell, everyone knows that. You're only half a man without her. I've known that since we first met all those years ago in California. Is she better today?" Luke asked.

"Yeah. She's stronger. She still gets disoriented. This morning she woke again thinking we were back in Scotland and wondered what had happened to the rooms. She remembered faster this time. She asked me three times to walk with her at the beach yesterday before I finally convinced her we weren't in California. Her memories seem to be jumbled. She's improving," Fox answered.

"If we can do anything to help, ask."

Fox nodded.

Kallik was at Draoithe working with the two horses, so it had freed up time for Javier to respond to immortal inquiries about the retreat, but he avoided his email inbox. They needed a front desk manager in a hurry.

"Hey guys, give me your opinions."

Isabell popped into the living room holding a painting. She had paint in her hair. She'd worked while talking with Eli and Artie in the solarium. Isabell showed them a painting of Andrei and Nadine.

"Something's wrong with Fangs, but I can't seem to get his vampire guise right. What do you see?" Isabell asked.

"You painted his eyes the way he always shows his fangs to you. When he switches guises, they turn red," Javier said.

"Are you sure?"

Isabell frowned at the painting with menace, as if the painting had made the mistake. Fox and Luke nodded.

CHAPTER TEN

A Good Idea

*L*uke

"Damn it. Okay, I can fix it." Isabell said.

"It's superb. Isabell, you're beyond talented. Will you paint Mihaela and Kallik next?" Luke asked.

Isabell had painted the couples as an art theme for the retreat.

"No, probably Ryker and Lily. I need to see Kallik and Mihaela more, mostly Kallik. I haven't seen his bear often enough to get it right, and I wouldn't want him angry with me."

Isabell laughed as she left to fix her painting.

"She has a good eye. This theme she's on will be good for Draoithe. She should hang these at the retreat," Fox suggested.

"Yeah, I don't think we can sell any of that. It's too personal for us. I hope she paints dragons, too," Luke said.

"After they're mated and bonded," Javier growled.

Luke and Fox laughed.

"Have we heard anything else about Elliot?" Luke asked.

"The warehouses burned out completely, just as you planned. None of my contacts have heard anything. No one seems to know where he is. Andrei has stopped working on the data entry project to comb through the hard drives he took from the warehouse. If he finds anything, I'll let you know. He refused to let Nadine work on it with him. He didn't want the images in her head. Artie's not allowed to view any of it, either. I'm afraid for her, she's too weak. Isabell still bursts into flames when people discuss Elliot near her."

Fox shook his head.

"Let me know when you get anything which might help us. I'd love to shut him down. More than that, ask Andrei to look for information on what they did to Griz. He has only intermittent control of his shifter magic. It's making him edgy. Melody wants to help him, but he may need a white witch," Luke said.

"Let's hope Melody can contain the situation until Artie is herself again. I won't risk her before she's healthy," Fox growled.

"Relax, my friend, I'd never risk Artie. I considered asking you to seek one for us. If things get worse, we may need to pay for a service," Luke said.

"I'll see what I can do. It won't come cheap," Fox said.

"Money isn't important," Javier said.

Luke nodded his concurrence. They would indeed spend the money well if Griz was the last Ruiri.

Griz

Griz had to get out of the house. He needed sunshine and fresh air. His ankle was much better that morning. The cane helped.

Melody had returned dressed from the restroom and helped him to stand. It took a minute, but he dressed himself. Breakfast was definitely in order first, but he looked forward to seeing the outdoors with a snowy owl.

He studied Melody as they made their way to the dining room. She wore faded jeans and a t-shirt that had seen better days. She was sexy and made the older clothing look too good, but Griz wondered about her financial situation.

She was young and not financially comfortable enough to dress the part. He would have to rectify her station in life. She should have better, finer things. His mate shouldn't dress so poorly.

Griz said nothing. He would need to get in touch with his bookkeeper soon and have replacement cards and identifications sent to him. He couldn't stay and court Melody in his current situation. Food first, then the land and the sky.

"Good morning sleepyheads," Nadine said.

"You look better today, Griz. Do you guys want waffles?"

"That sounds good."

Griz smiled at Nadine.

Melody had filled him in on some people. Nadine suffered from insomnia. She made breakfast in the mornings after the sun called to Andrei unless she'd crashed.

No one woke her if she fell asleep somewhere. They usually covered her with a blanket and waited until Andrei found her and carried her off to bed.

Nadine had two platters of hot waffles on the table. The honey, syrup, whipped cream, and butter were sitting next to bowls of fresh clean blueberries, blackberries, strawberries, and diced peaches.

Griz's mouth watered. Melody handed Griz a plate, napkin, and silverware and asked what he wanted to drink.

"Breakfast tea please, and thank you, Melody. I appreciate the help."

He smiled up at her.

It felt nice to have her take care of him. No woman had done that since his mother passed long ago. Melody made him happy with the little things she did for him. Maybe no one else would notice, but Griz did.

She'd helped him before they ever met. She was too good for him. He knew it instantly, but he wouldn't let her go. He couldn't do it. Griz needed her. She was *everything*.

They sat and ate breakfast. Artie, Isabell, and Eli joined them. He heard Luke, Javier, and Fox talking in the living room. The house was full of people.

"How do you feel today, Griz?" Isabell asked.

"Much better today. Thank you. I think if Melody will accompany me, I'd like to get outside today," Griz said.

"There's a creek behind the gazebo out back, Melody. Maybe take a walk that way. If you get tired, you can sit and rest before coming back," Artie suggested.

Griz perked up at that. Water drew the bear. Running water meant fishing. Griz pushed the bear's sentimentality back. He was already eating. It was ridiculous sometimes.

"Are you guys comfortable?" Nadine asked.

Griz looked at Melody. Was she comfortable? He didn't care if he was comfortable.

"We're fine. The room is perfect. Thank you."

Melody smiled. Griz relaxed. He hadn't realized her answer was so important until after she spoke.

"We all want you to stay, Melody. Is there any question we could answer for you?" Artie asked.

Griz noted Artie spoke to Melody and the other ladies. She was also a submissive then. He was an unmated male, and she didn't feel comfortable with him. She hadn't spoken to him in the dream, either.

He hadn't been around many shifters. The few he'd known had at least been open enough with him to share information about animal nature with him.

He'd learned about mating and bonding. Griz knew to seek Melody. He'd found her. She was all he wanted.

"Can you explain what a Ri ruirech and a Ruiri are?"

Melody asked a question. Griz wanted the answer as well. He continued eating waffles and listened to Artie explain the hierarchy system at Draoithe. A lot of magic floated around, but he felt no evil.

As breakfast ended, Griz spoke to Artie.

"I'm glad you're feeling better, Artie. Follow the rules. You'll be your old self in a couple of weeks."

"Thank you for helping me."

Artie looked away from him.

"You're quite welcome."

Griz smiled. Melody took both hers and Griz's plates and cups to the sink and rinsed everything and placed it in the dishwasher.

"Nadine, breakfast was excellent. Thank you for the waffles," Griz said, and everyone else echoed him.

"No problem. Breakfast is my specialty. I'll be working on the data entry if anyone needs me," Nadine said.

"I'll join you and help a bit," Artie said.

"No, you won't. Fox will kill me if he catches you working while you're supposed to be resting."

Nadine laughed on her way out to the garage workspace.

"Come, keep me company while I paint," Isabell said.

"Eli's coming too."

"Okay, I still feel a bit out of sorts. I don't want to be alone, but Fox needs to work. He gets aggravated when his routine gets messed up too often. I'm bothering him too much."

Artie explained, whiny. She was a fox. Griz sympathized with her. He, too, felt as if he were a burden.

"You're everything to Fox, Artie. Everybody knows that. But he's a bit alpha, and his work matters to him. He wants to do his job well. Same as you. You're just on medical leave. I'm on vacation. Come, relax with me."

Eli convinced Artie.

Griz rose to his feet as the women left. Melody handed him the cane, then took his arm as they made their way slowly out to the creek. The air felt good. It was already warm, and the afternoon would be hot.

The sky was blue; the grass was green, and the air smelled of the forest. Outdoors always spoke to the bear inside.

"Thank you for walking with me. I need a more open concept. I need a lot of windows and light to stay indoors. The vampires make the heavy drapes a necessity, but it still weighs on me."

"I imagine working outdoors so much would make you claustrophobic. I prefer the outdoors around moonrise myself. The sun is bright for me."

She wore dark sunglasses. She was an owl. Griz wanted to see her in the moonrise. He bet her hair would shine with it.

He would ask her to walk with him again to see that. Griz wanted to see her fly, too. He didn't like heights, but he imagined Melody would love them.

"I wanted to ask you, what do you think about Draoithe now?"

Melody asked Griz.

"It makes more sense to me. There's a lot of magic floating around. Even the vampires are more than just vampires, it seems. They have a quality of life here. These people are a lot like me. I was born a dreamwalker and a bear. Luke uses the pack bond to organize all these people, and he uses the fealty oath magic to strengthen his ruling council, ensuring he doesn't deal with treason. He's smart enough to employ people in meaningful work as well."

Griz liked the people.

"Why do you say that?"

"When people have meaningful work, they have a place they fit. They enjoy themselves and take pride in what they do. Even if things go wrong, if you have a suitable position, you won't leave it. You'll stay and work out the problems."

"He makes offers which will make them stay and build their working life. The people stay, they do what they love, it matters to others around them, and they feel at home."

Melody nodded as she summed up Griz's thoughts.

"Exactly! I bet he's done the same for sanctuary guests who needed therapy in the past and had success. It wouldn't surprise me if he does the same for the women he rescued from those warehouses. It's a good idea."

CHAPTER ELEVEN

Darker Grey

G *riz*

Griz admired Luke. The man was a leader of men. He gave orders, but he wanted to be smart about them. He didn't seek power. It just seemed to find Luke. He didn't like to have to make snap decisions, and Griz appreciated that.

Luke preferred as much information as possible, and he valued the opinions of others who were equally intelligent. Griz operated like that as well. The more information he had, the easier it was to see the path in the stillness.

Luke had asked Griz questions about barns and cattle when he realized Griz was knowledgeable. Eli had done the same to a lesser extent and so had Javier.

Isabell had been more of a giver of information to balance the questions the others had. She'd kept the conversation going.

If Griz had to guess, the phoenix had once been a sanctuary guest. She'd identified with Griz's plight, even though she theoretically played for the other team.

"It's not enough to make you want to stay, though, is it?" Melody asked.

Griz knew she wanted to stay. He needed to know more. He couldn't make a snap decision.

"I like what Luke is doing. But you're correct in your assessment of my independent lifestyle. I'd need to see the land Draoithe offers and hear an offer that appealed to me before I would say 'yes'. To reinvent myself and liquidate my holdings in Colorado, I'd need more convincing."

Griz spoke honestly as they walked along the edge of the creek.

When Griz looked up, a man and a woman had stepped off the porch of the neighboring house and came towards them. Griz stopped walking and shifted his weight onto his good ankle as he waited for the couple to greet them.

As the two came closer, Griz could see the man focused on Melody. Griz didn't like it. He didn't want any man looking at his mate. It irritated the bear, and Griz already had issues with that.

When the man stopped in front of them, Griz could see a leather thong around the man's neck showing in his open shirt collar. Griz studied the man through the dream. The man wore a collar along with others. Necromancy.

Griz rumbled low at the newcomer. The man ignored the warning. He looked at Melody instead. He shouldn't have.

Grizzly bears fought to the death over their mates. Griz felt more bear than a man standing next to Melody.

"My Lady, I'm Smoke. It's a pleasure to meet you. Lightning suggested you were in residence, but occupied with another mission. We haven't met the other guests at Draoithe."

Smoke offered a gallant bow and a smile.

Griz rumbled again, and Melody took a step back in answer to Griz's warning. Smoke looked a bit confused. Griz didn't want the dark art spawn near Melody.

All necromancy felt wrong to dreamwalkers. The grey dragon wasn't in the dream properly. His soul had divided, and he wasn't fully present in the dream.

"She's not your lady, and you seem to have a lot of information about *my* lady for someone she's never met."

"She's my queen, sir. I don't think I like your tone."

Smoke turned to face Griz.

Smoke didn't like his tone? Really? Was he challenging Griz for Melody? He would lose that fight.

The little brown-haired woman tried to get Smoke's attention, but he just shrugged her hand off his arm. Griz didn't like that either.

Smoke should pay attention to the woman. He brought her with him. He should've shown more respect. That made the encounter worse.

"No, she's my mate. You're the product of some foul magic. Do not come any closer to her. I won't have you harm her."

Griz rumbled the warning at Smoke again. The man ignored him.

Smoke turned back toward Melody again.

"My queen, are you in danger? Do you need help?"

Smoke questioned Griz's mate about her safety in front of him.

The anger which had built inside Griz ever since he woke up in a cage in a warehouse took over. Griz saw red. The flames traced over the big man.

Whatever had been blocking him from shifting into his grizzly bear's form had ceased. Griz, in his bear's form, towered above Smoke at over nine feet tall.

Griz roared at Smoke. He would protect his mate from the evil which threatened her.

Smoke tried to reach for Melody. She cowered behind Griz. The flames traced her into a snowy owl, and she stepped away and into the sky. Griz stepped into the stillness of the inverted dream to see the path he should take.

He focused on Smoke as soon as Melody traced and swiped a massive clawed paw at him. Strangely, his paw was black instead of brown.

It was odd, but Griz didn't puzzle it out. Smoke backed away, so Griz stepped through the dream faster than Smoke could move. He wouldn't be reaching for Melody ever again.

Griz's paw ripped the man's throat open. Smoke sank wide-eyed to his knees as his blood colored his shirt red.

Griz fell forward onto his front paws and mauled Smoke until the man didn't move. Blood covered Griz's silver-streaked grizzled fur, staining it pink.

Griz snuffled Smoke to be sure he was dead, then looked up to see the little brown-haired woman crying.

Griz felt sorrow for her. She seemed hurt by Smoke's demise, but Griz wasn't upset. Melody was safe.

No man would touch his mate. Grizzly bears didn't share what belonged to them.

He backed away from Smoke's mangled, blood-stained body to look for Melody. He shook the gore from his coat, flinging the stench of the necromancy from him. The blood steamed and turned to ash.

The brown-haired woman knelt next to Smoke and wept. The grizzly bear could offer no sympathy. It was his mate who concerned him.

Griz found Melody in a nearby tree. He snuffled up at her and sank to the ground beneath the tree to await her. She landed silently next to him and rubbed her small white owl head against his bear's cheek. She was safe.

Griz had protected her. He extended his paw, and she perched on it as she had in the dream. He laid his head down on his other paw to rest. Tired, he still wouldn't let anything touch his owl.

She wanted to be near him. She wanted the protection he offered her. He gave it to her.

It was eleven o'clock in the morning. Fox, Javier, Luke, Eli, Isabell, Artie, and Ash ran across the grass from Fox's house while a little auburn-haired girl raced to the brown-haired woman's side from the neighboring house.

The men reached the scene first. Javier was quick to note Smoke was dead and shifted immediately into his enormous black direwolf. The phoenix flames dripped from his fangs as he placed himself between Griz and Luke.

Ash grabbed the two women who had knelt beside Smoke and dragged them back to the other women.

"Stay here. His return will disorient him. It's okay. He'll return. Fox won't leave his friend in the Netherworld," Ash said.

Fox touched Luke on the arm and pointed at Griz and Melody. Luke put his hand on Javier's wolf's shoulder as he moved toward Griz and Melody.

Fox turned back and made the druid fire after he knew Isabell had moved Artie farther away from him. He touched the dead man on the forehead and let the magic go. It covered Smoke's body and put it back to rights.

When the magic seemed to soak into the repaired corpse, Fox spoke Smoke's real name, and Smoke caught his breath. The soul of Maddox Talog returned to the Leaindeail.

The black and purple flames traced over his body, and he rose from the ground as a great grey dragon. His scales were a bluish-grey color and his hair, horns, tail spikes, and wing bones were a couple of shades of darker grey.

CHAPTER TWELVE

To Protect Her

G*riz*

Smoke pointed his snout toward the sky and let the dragon flame go with a great bellow of fury. He turned toward Griz. There was no longer any question for Griz about what Javier had meant by dragons.

Smoke had a wicked dragon grin with razor-sharp pointed teeth, and the smoke curled up from his nostrils. He picked up one foot to go after Griz, but stopped when he heard Fox's question.

"Would you break your oath, dragon? Would you harm a Ruiri of the realm? Is your honor worth so little?"

Fox badgered Smoke, and the dragon hung his head. He wouldn't dishonor himself. Fox turned to Keira.

"I apologize for being late. I got your message. Thank you. We haven't formally met. I'm Duncan O'Sullivan. You must be Keira Behrnun. It's a pleasure to meet you, ma'am. I'm afraid Smoke needs a woman's guidance. He was always the hotheaded type. We've been friends for centuries, and he behaves larger than he is."

Fox smiled at the brown-haired woman as she wiped her tears away.

Eli walked past the two women, a dragon, and Fox, grumbling something about neighbors, and caught up with Luke and Javier carrying a small stack of clothes in her arms.

Griz, are you hurt?

Luke spoke in his head. How did he do that? He wasn't a dream walker. Griz lifted his bear's head and tilted it, looking at Luke, puzzled, but he answered.

Luke, your dreamtalk has the same volume as your aura.

Griz chuckled.

I'm unharmed. Melody's safe. Tell your dragon to keep his hands off my mate. I won't share what is mine. He should still be dead.

Luke looked back at the others.

"Smoke, did you try to touch Melody?"

Smoke looked away.

"He reached for her when the bear shifted. He feared for her safety," Keira answered.

Luke grumbled something about needing the money dragons hoarded to clean up their messes. That explained the money situation Griz had wondered about. Luke looked back at Smoke and spoke down to the dragon.

"I swear I feel like I'm running a shifter kindergarten. Why would you reach for another shifter's mate? Are you insane? The man's a dreamwalker and a grizzly bear. I know of one who ran down a four-hundred-year-old vampire. You could never have matched Griz's speed unless you turn into Andrei. Whatever you thought, it was a bad idea. I swear everybody takes fucking classes at the university and learns about everybody else," Luke fumed.

Draoithe had a diverse collection of immortals. More education on their quirks would probably be a good idea, given the amount of magic Luke curated.

"Who would've thought being Ri ruirech meant I had to mediate between two boys on the playground fighting over a pretty girl?"

"Boys don't change."

Eli laughed.

She dropped a pair of pants in front of Javier and pointed to the woods. Javier whined at her, wagged his tail, picked up the pants in his teeth, and bounded into the trees.

"Smoke, get cleaned up. You need to escort Keira to Fox's library at one o'clock. You can explain yourself then," Luke commanded.

Isabell had drawn Artie away from Fox and stood with Ash and Raven in the gazebo out of the sun. Fox hadn't wanted his mate close to the magic he'd used to bring Smoke back.

Luke faced Griz again.

Griz, can you trace? Can you shift?

Yeah, I think so. I need to rest. I got too angry. It took a lot of energy to shift. It felt different. Like I learned a new way to make the magic obey my thoughts. May I ask Eli something?

She can hear you.

Griz looked at Eli. Luke had gained the dreamtalk because of his bond with Eli. She was the tiger in the dreamwalk with Artie. The puzzle pieces clicked together in Griz's mind.

Ah, so she's how you dreamtalk. Eli, will you discuss what happened today with Kallik? I would know his thoughts and invite him to meet me in the dream? I would like to know if my dream is wrong.

I will. I have clothes for you and Melody. Shall I leave them in the Gazebo?

Yes, please. When Melody is ready, I'll guard her privacy. No harm will harm her. She is everything.

Luke, what did Fox mean when he asked Smoke if he would harm a Ruiri?

I want you as a guardian of the realm. I'd hoped to wait until you were healthier to speak with you about it. The dragons are protectors of the realm. They swore a fealty oath to serve me and my Ruiri. You don't have to accept the position. It has to be your choice. If Smoke had attacked you, I would've punished him. The magic sees you as I see you. It would've demanded justice.

Isabell, Artie, and Fox collected the remnants of tattered clothes from the lawn as Javier walked out of the woods in loose joggers. Ash and Raven followed them, whispering as they made their way back to Fox's house.

I'll consider it. I want to apologize for striking down your man. He was foolish to anger the bear in me. I'm still weak, but I should have thought it out first.

Forget it. He tried to reach for your mate. He's a shifter. Smoke knew better than to do that. You sustained injuries as well. I can't be angry with you any more than I was angry with the panther who killed my lieutenant.

Griz blinked. A panther killed his lieutenant?

He tried to piss on a wounded black panther. She attacked him and almost killed him when Andrei saved him from her and had to turn him into a vampire to keep him from dying. Javier and I went after the panther when I realized she was a shifter. It turned out well in the end.

The place got crazier by the minute.

Yeah, the panther recognized the man as her mate and claimed him a week later.

Eli illuminated the situation.

Try living here. It can be interesting.

Luke and Eli both laughed as they turned to walk back to Fox's house.

He waited for Melody to dress. She wore a simple sundress, but the quality was much higher than the clothes she'd worn when she shifted and ruined her outfit. Her tennis shoes remained intact, but they showed signs of wear.

Griz pulled on the pair of joggers Eli left for him and tried not to stare at Melody. She was even sexier than he'd thought before. It was making his heart beat too fast.

Griz could feel Melody's eyes on his back when he straightened up. She hadn't seen him without an undershirt before.

She could see the tattoo of his last name, Locklear, in old English letters across his shoulders. His wounds had all closed and scarred over.

There was some bruising left, but most had faded to yellow. He felt good standing in the sun as he stepped out of the gazebo toward her.

"You look better today."

Melody squeaked when she realized he knew she gawked at him and waited for her to look her fill.

Griz chuckled. She was young.

"Do you like what you see?" He asked her.

He felt a million times more relaxed, knowing he could shift again. Melody blushed and looked away from him.

Griz stepped up close to her.

"Melody, please look at me."

Melody looked up at his face.

"It's okay for you to look at me. I'm glad my mate finds me physically attractive. I have a hard time keeping my eyes off of you because I think you're beautiful. Perhaps you won't be angry with me if you catch me staring?"

Melody smiled at him as she blushed. Griz fell into her and got lost. She was so small. He wanted to protect her.

CHAPTER THIRTEEN

Clicked The Play Button

G^{riz}

Would she let him kiss her? Just one taste. He would be in heaven if she did.

His head moved toward her. He felt her fingers slide around his neck, pulling him down to her.

Griz closed his eyes as their lips touched. Melody's lips were soft. His lips moved over hers, carefully memorizing the way they felt.

His arms circled her waist as he drew her body closer to his. He wanted to feel her heart close to him.

She smelled like *gardenia*. Her feminine feel spoke to him on a deep physical level. He needed Melody.

She was his mate. He had found her. He wanted to mark her and claim her.

It was too soon. They were too new to each other. Just the first light kiss had his heart rate too high.

His being breathed for one woman. He lost himself in her. Time stopped.

Griz kissed Melody long and slowly. When he pulled back to let her breathe, she sighed in sheer joy. She opened her eyes and smiled shyly at him.

Griz fell, lost to her. Whatever she ever asked of him, he would do for her. She was everything.

She gave him back to himself.

"That was unreal. I've never experienced a kiss like that before."

"I've never kissed a woman like you before. You're unbelievably amazing to me. I couldn't allow that dragon to touch you because I have to have you for myself. I'll never hurt you or pressure you for anything you would say no, but no other man can have what's mine. You're mine."

Griz rumbled at her, still holding her close. She needed to know how he felt.

"Will you always protect me, Griz? I'm not strong like you."

She was still a little breathless.

"I'll always protect you, Snowbird. I need you with me. You saved me. My strength is yours."

"Then I wish to be yours."

Griz picked her up and hugged her as he spun her around. He set her down laughing. He grinned at her.

He realized her eyes watered in the bright sunlight. She'd lost her dark glasses when she shifted. He should take her back inside.

"Shall we head back to the house? I think you need to get out of the sun before you burn. I need to find a phone, so I can make some calls. If I can borrow a car, how would you feel about taking a drive? We could explore some of the city?"

Melody nodded.

They walked back to Fox's and slipped into the room without running into anyone.

"I need clothes."

He wasn't ungrateful to Kallik, quite the contrary. Still, he needed things to his taste, which fit a little better. Kallik was larger than Griz.

He grabbed some things as he set the boots down. They didn't work with joggers, so he'd carried them back.

"Let me get changed and wash up, and I'll see about a phone and us getting out of here, okay?"

She smiled at him.

He limped down the hall to the restroom. The ankle healed rapidly with all the food he'd eaten. It took him a few minutes to get dressed properly, but he felt better.

Griz wished he knew where the damn cane went. He'd lost it when he shifted. He'd have to go back and look for it.

He stepped out of the restroom and practically ran into the most beautiful man he'd ever seen. He tried to back up too fast and almost lost his balance before catching himself on the doorframe.

"You must be Enyeto Locklear. It's nice to meet you. I'm Andrei Alexandrescu."

The pretty slender man had a heavy eastern European accent. He sounded a little like Dracula from the movies. His voice was soft. His soul was only a sliver in the dream. He had accepted the dark gift and paid the price. He was a vampire. The man held out his hand, and Griz shook it.

"I am. Please, call me Griz. It's nice to meet you, Andrei. Am I in your way? I was on my way out. It's all yours."

Griz gestured to the empty bathroom.

"No, I was looking for you. I have some things you might want. I went with Luke on the raid of those warehouses. My role was to take anything personal or magical and anything of intellectual value. The women had nothing, but interestingly enough, I found this wallet."

Andrei pulled Griz's wallet from his pocket and handed it over.

"Luke requested I put money in it in case they stole yours. I hope a thousand dollars will cover anything you may have lost. Your driver's license and bank cards were still in it. You may wish to check for anything else amiss."

Griz opened his wallet. All of his bank cards were there, along with his driver's license and a few business cards. There were a thousand dollars in cash as well.

"I don't know what to say. Thank you. The cash is too much, let me return it. You didn't take my money. Why should you replace it?"

Griz took the money out of his wallet to give it back.

"Luke said you would say that."

Andrei laughed, refusing him.

"He said to tell you to keep it in case you need it. If you decide to stay on with us, he'll work out a trade with you later."

Griz put the money back in his wallet and nodded. Andrei took out two new cell phones from his pocket and handed them to Griz.

"One's for Melody, and the other is for your use. Nadine programmed them both with the phone numbers of all the council members in case you have any issues or questions. Vampires and Lily are unlikely to answer from dawn until late afternoon. Nadine keeps odd hours, but the rest are usually available during the day. Luke asks if you choose to leave, please leave the phones behind. He hopes you will stay, as do I."

"He's giving us phones?"

"All Druid pack members, council members, oath sworn, dragonsworn, and the Druid pack provide all sanctuary guests with communications. Just in case someone gets lost. Oh, the number to Melody's man is on the phone as well. Just text and her servant will assist you if you need something."

"Melody's man?"

He felt like he only repeated what Andrei said. The pretty man piled up the information Griz needed to know.

"The dragonsworn disrespected women and became servants. Stripped of their former identities, they have assignments to serve a woman according to the tiger's decree. The one you roared at last night serves Melody, and by extension, does what you say. Should he displease either of you, simply have her tell him, and he'll confess to the dragons for punishment on Friday at sunset."

Andrei smiled a wicked grin.

The pretty man seemed happy with the servant's arrangement. Griz didn't know Andrei, but he liked the way the man thought.

"Okay, thank you, Andrei. I appreciate it."

"No problem. I have to get to work, but I found something I think you need to see from the video feed at the warehouse. Have you got a minute?"

Griz nodded.

"I wanted to show you while Melody isn't around, and I won't show it to Nadine. I don't think the ladies need to see. It might be too much. I preferred to shield my consort. She already suffers from nightmares and insomnia."

Andrei had lowered his already low voice on that last part.

"Gotcha. Lead the way."

Griz followed Andrei down the hallway to the garage-turned-computer workspace.

"I want to warn you some of the stuff is graphic. Luke said he preferred to ask you about it rather than subjecting any of the rescued women to it. Are you up for it?"

"Yeah, I can handle it. I agree with Luke's assessment."

Griz didn't think it would be right to subject the women to any more trauma.

Andrei wanted to know if Griz could make any identifications, or if seeing any video feed might jog his memory about what happened in the warehouses and why.

They stepped up to an open laptop on a counter, and Andrei typed in a password. There was a paused video feed on the screen.

Andrei looked at Griz. Griz nodded, and Andrei clicked the play button.

CHAPTER FOURTEEN

A Few Calls

G*riz*

Griz saw a large naked man wearing only a gold cap on his penis with thin gold chains wrapping around his shaft attached to a rather tight-fitting gold cockring. If he didn't know what was about to happen, he would've thought it was a scene out of a BDSM porn flick.

"Do you know this man? Do you recognize him?" Andrei asked.

"He was there when the women came in. I don't know his name. I think I was there first. The day I regained consciousness was the only time I saw him. He was the breaker. The others used the women on a timed schedule after he broke them."

Griz closed his eyes.

One by one, they brought the women to the man. They were all naked and struggled to get away.

The man had a method to make them more docile. He would slam them against a wall and hold them off the floor by pinning their wrists above their head so their toes barely touched the floor.

He waited until the fight drained out of them, as they needed to support their weight. He positioned himself in front of them and rape them until they slumped unconscious and bloody to the floor when he released them.

It was hard to remember. The man didn't even get off on it. It was like a job. He just broke them.

Griz was too weak to do anything except watch. He listened as the women begged and screamed.

On the third woman, a man stepped into the room to see if the breaker was ready for the next woman. He'd asked the breaker a question.

"Hey, Rake, are you ready for the next one?"

"Yeah, bring her. This one's done for."

Rake had slid out of the woman and let her crumple up on the floor.

Rake brutalized ten women in front of Griz, and Griz could do nothing to stop it. His anger rose again. He had control.

"They called him 'Rake'. That's all I know. Sorry, man," Griz said.

Andrei noted it on a pad of paper and didn't ask for more. He'd seen the video. He'd already seen what Griz had seen, and Andrei didn't need the sound bytes, only the name.

"Don't worry. Fox is good. It might take a bit, but we'll find him. Luke wants him. He gave standing orders to the dragons to take him alive if they caught him. He'll become dragonsworn, and his job is to clean and maintain the toilets and the sewage lines at Draoithe. Luke mentioned something about attaching the contraption between his legs, so he jingles when he walks after the dragons remove his masculinity. The Inner Circle endorsed the orders."

Andrei smiled an evil smile. Griz liked the vampire.

Andrei closed the window and opened another on the computer to show Griz a different scene. They injected Griz with syringes filled with drugs. He was in his bear form. Griz rumbled at the scene.

"What was it? What did they give me?"

"We think they were shooting you full of testosterone and cocaine. They worked on the theory that high levels of testosterone combined with cocaine would block your ability to shift. If they could damage the part of your brain which controls testosterone levels in men by combining the testosterone with the cocaine, they were hoping to send your shifter magic into permanent hibernation."

Andrei talked as they watched the scene progress.

He watched as his body convulsed in seizures. When the spasms stopped, they injected him again, and he seized again. Andrei pushed the pause button. Griz stared at the screen.

"How many times?"

"Three times an hour for three hours. Five days in a row until you went comatose. Your body shut down. You shifted into your bear on the second day and didn't shift back until you came here."

Why was he not dead? He had to say it out loud.

"How am I not dead? How do I even know who I am?"

"I don't know, but as near as any of us can figure, now that you are no longer comatose and aren't having seizures, you're suffering from confusion, malnutrition, and a serious case of steroid-induced aggression which I think is wearing off since you seemed to have overextended yourself by protecting Melody and killing a dragon. What do I know? I'm a vampire, not a doctor."

Andrei grinned. Griz laughed.

"Having said that. I would suggest recreational cocaine not be something you do in the future, and unless my sources were wrong about you kissing Melody this afternoon at the gazebo, I'm going out on a limb and suggesting testosterone replacement therapy isn't necessary, either."

"Are you guys spying on me?!"

"Add paranoia to the list of suffering side effects. No, bro. The two of you occupied Javier's preferred destination for his midday marijuana high."

Andrei laughed.

"His Druid magic seems to work better for him if he gets high first. He goes out to the gazebo to practice, so he doesn't accidentally damage the house. He's powerful. Fox is his only match."

Griz laughed at that. He could envision it after having seen Javier as his direwolf with the phoenix flames. Adding another magic would make Javier a dangerous enemy. It was nice to know Javier worked for Luke and not against him.

"Can I help you with anything else?"

"Do you remember how they took you? There's no video feed on that. The cameras didn't start rolling until they had already beaten and locked you down under sedation."

Andrei noted the hole in their attempt to recreate the events which happened to Griz and the women. Griz was thankful for the knowledge Andrei had shared with him.

"No. I had a drink at my favorite bar in Boulder. It's still fuzzy."

"Well, if anything comes to you, let one of us know and we'll add it to the stack of information we're amassing to solve this puzzle. Luke wants to send a message and disabling Elliot's kidnapping ring is the focus. The smallest things sometimes turn out to be the biggest clues."

"I want a reckoning for myself. I'll let you know if I figure something out."

Griz would like to do some harm to Elliot.

"Hey, what if I needed a car to get out and see a movie or go to the mall? I want to take Melody out for a bit," Griz asked.

"I don't go out much. Talk to Ryker. He's the garage foreman. Ryker keeps up with cars and trucks. He would know. Tell him you can borrow my Hummer. I don't drive it often, so I won't miss it. I run faster than I can drive, and I can teleport anywhere I've been before."

Andrei shrugged his shoulders.

"Okay, thanks again."

"If you need anything else, or think of anything that might help the investigation, text me. I'm still looking through the video feed for the other warehouse, but so far nothing useful has appeared. Nadine's waking up. Gotta go."

Andrei smiled, and he winked out of the garage.

He simply disappeared. Griz blinked and stuck his hand into the air where the vampire had stood. Just air. Weird.

Griz limped down the hall. He knocked on the door and entered when Melody spoke from the other side.

"Are you okay? You were gone for a long time," Melody asked.

"I ran into Andrei in the hallway. He gave me back my wallet. Seems he found it at the warehouse the night they rescued me. He also gave me two cell phones from Luke. Luke said they're for us to use while we're here. We have to see Ryker, and we can borrow Andrei's Hummer. He doesn't drive much and says he won't miss it."

Griz grinned as he handed Melody the phone.

"Javier stopped and left your cane. He said he found it out by the gazebo."

"Oh, good. I thought I'd lost it."

Griz took the cane from her hand. Javier must have gotten high after all.

Melody scrolled through the phone.

"They have you here twice because you're listed as Griz and Melody's man. Wait, who's Melody's man?"

Melody giggled until she realized the numbers weren't the same.

"We have a servant assigned to you. All the women have one. If you need anything, you can text him, and he'll help. If he doesn't do his job well, you tell him, and he'll confess to a dragon to be punished. They have to serve a woman because of their guilt at mistreating a woman."

Melody cringed.

"They have sexual predators as servants?"

"No, they're gelded and turned as dragonsworn. They lack the equipment to harm a woman."

Griz tried to explain it delicately.

"That's creepy. Just when I liked the place, leave it to the dragons to mess it up again."

Melody shuddered.

Griz shrugged. He'd thought it might be the dragons' only redeeming quality. He wasn't too keen on dragons after that morning. Feeling much better, Griz thought he could let the incident go, so long as it never repeated.

"Let me make a few calls, then we'll find Ryker and see something different."

Melody grinned at him and set her phone up with the apps she wanted, while Griz made a few calls.

CHAPTER FIFTEEN

Clothes And Shopping

G^{riz}

His boss at the ranch was happy to hear from him, but sad to tell him he'd hired someone to take his place because he'd been gone for almost a month.

It was nearly time to reinvent himself, anyway. Griz asked to have his saddle shipped to him instead of his last paycheck. His old boss took down the address and agreed.

Replacing his saddle would cost more than his last check. Shipping it would be cheaper than paying Griz. It was a win on both sides.

Griz had enough money to see him through any rough patch. He wasn't independently wealthy, but he had needed little and saved most of his earnings over the years. He could easily afford to court his snowy owl rather handsomely.

When Griz and Melody made it to the garage at Eli's house, it was only about three-thirty in the afternoon. As his left leg hobbled him, driving wasn't a problem.

Griz knocked on the side door. He barely heard the reply. He opened the door to find a man standing completely in the shadows. Griz closed the door, and the room went black. Then the lights came on.

"Sorry about that. The sun is detrimental to my current health situation. What can I do for you?" the man asked them.

He spoke quietly as Andrei had but without a foreign accent, and he looked like a male model. The man was too pretty for a man. He must be a vampire, too.

Griz studied the man in the dream for a moment. He was a vampire and something odd.

Griz shook his head and put out his hand to the man.

"I'm Griz, and this is Melody. I'm looking for a man named Ryker about a car?"

"I'm Ryker, and it's nice to meet you. Which vehicle did you need?"

Ryker smiled at Melody, but immediately focused on Griz.

The man was smart. Griz didn't particularly care for other men looking at Melody, because she was his.

"Andrei said we might borrow his Hummer. We'll return it before midnight."

Griz assured Ryker.

"As long as I get it back before dawn. Luke's a bit frustrated with the parking situation at the moment."

Ryker grinned.

"When they finish the garage at Draoithe, things will be easier."

"Thanks, we appreciate it," Griz said.

Ryker handed him the keys and pointed to a black Hummer.

"Would you mind answering a personal question?" Griz asked.

There was just something off about the man.

"Panther. Best mistake I ever made. She is *everything*."

Ryker grinned.

He switched guises so Griz could see his elliptical pupils.

"Sorry to bother you. It confused the dreamwalker in me," Griz said.

"Yeah, I get that look from Eli and Kallik, too. I figured. The dragons I've met look at me as a dog looks at a cellphone which speaks with its owner's voice. It's been... interesting."

Ryker laughed.

Griz had to hand it to the guy. He had comfort in his own skin.

He must be the lieutenant Luke had spoken of earlier. Griz liked the man instantly. Any man who laughed at dragons had to be a decent sort.

"Give me a minute before you hit the garage door opener. If you don't mind, click it again once you back out. Otherwise, it will waste a few hours for me."

"You got it. Thanks," Griz said.

Melody smiled when Ryker nodded, then the man winked out of existence. Melody stared at the space he'd been in.

"Andrei did that to me earlier. It's odd."

"It feels like a magic trick. I wonder how they do it?"

"I dunno. That might have to get on the list of things we need to learn. This place is growing on me. These people seem legitimate. Shall we see something different?"

Melody smiled at him.

Griz helped her into the passenger side, then he climbed into the driver's seat and adjusted the seat and mirrors. He hit the garage door opener before he started the engine. They waited until the door was up and backed out of the garage.

Griz hit the garage door button again as they cleared the door. He made sure it came down, then backed out of the driveway.

"What would you like to see, snowbird?"

"Tyler is the Rose Capital of the World. Can we see their rose garden?"

"Do you have it programmed into Google Maps?"

Griz smiled knowingly. Melody nodded shyly.

"One rose garden coming up."

Griz drove, as the phone intoned the driving directions, feeling much better than he had in over a month. Melody made the dream brighter for him.

"What would you like for dinner?"

"Oh, Griz, I don't have enough money to eat out. We don't have to eat out. I can wait until we return," Melody said.

Griz almost rumbled his dissatisfaction with her answer before he remembered her age. Young men didn't know how to treat a woman and the women didn't know what they should expect from a man. His mother had made sure Griz knew how to treat a woman.

Men paid. Women were beautiful company.

"Melody, I'm not one of those fools you went to college with. I've never asked a woman out and expected her to pay, nor have I ever taken money from a woman. I think we need that straight between us first. You're my mate. I wouldn't have sought you if I couldn't provide for you. Do you understand?"

Griz asked her kindly, but on that topic, he wouldn't budge.

"Okay, I think so. It feels strange to me. No one ever took care of me before, Griz."

Griz nodded. That was how it should be. He wanted to be the one who took care of her.

"Don't accept gifts from other men, Melody. Unless you would like the man to disappear. In that case, by all means. I'll see to his demise. The bear in me needs to take care of you, but I can't share you with any others. If you need something from me, name it, and you'll have it."

"Okay. I think. Thanks for talking to Ryker. I'm not comfortable talking to men. I prefer to speak with women. They're less... overpowering."

Melody relaxed. Griz smiled. She was a true submissive. He didn't mind if she didn't want to talk with the men at Draoithe. He preferred it that way.

"I want to work, Griz. I like to play with the cloth to make clothes and things. If we stay, I want to take the job Luke offered."

Griz liked how she'd decided his decision was her decision as well. He wanted to feel the team concept in their relationship. It should be a joint decision.

"I know. I have no issue with that. What you earn will always be yours. I don't wish to cage you. It's that I need you so bad I can't allow another to take you from me or harm you."

He never wanted her to lose her freedom. If a wild bird couldn't fly, it was no longer beautiful. No one would ever cage his owl. She would always fly. And his need for her grew with his increasing health and vitality. The bear wanted its mate.

"Thanks, Griz. That matters to me. I appreciate that. What about a Chinese buffet? We can have some of everything, and we can eat all we need," Melody suggested.

Griz knew she wanted to soothe his ruffled feathers. She was too good to be true.

"Now you're speaking to the bear in me, darlin'. A rose garden and some good Chinese food sound like the plan. I don't know how much walking I can do, but I heard about an outlet mall in Tyler where you can drive up to the storefronts. Shall we go? I need a few things. If you see anything you like, we'll grab that, too."

"Are you taking me shopping?" Melody asked.

Her eyes lit up. She was a woman, after all. She was a fashion designer. Maybe he could win her even if he was a broken old bear. Clothes and shopping seemed like her idea of a date.

CHAPTER SIXTEEN

Needed To Meditate

Griz

"Sure, why not? Kallik's clothes don't fit me well. I need some clothes. I prefer jeans to dress slacks, and I need heavy cotton dress shirts. That broadcloth thin stuff doesn't last. I seem to have lost my hat and my belt. The boots Kallik gave me are nice, but everything else feels wrong. I need something normal. If all you have is what's in your suitcase, then I figure you could use a few items too. So does it sound okay?"

It was probably not the best first date, but the most practical one. He wasn't much for the romantic stuff. He was far more of a realist, but he wasn't a fool, either.

Almost all women liked to shop, and his Snowbird liked clothes. He bet she liked shoes, purses, and accessories just as much. Maybe he would find a jewelry store next to a good men's store.

The rose garden was beautiful. Griz didn't mind admitting he liked the pretty flowers. His new favorite flower was gardenia. Melody smelled like *gardenia,* and he'd smelled nothing so seductive.

There were a few benches in the garden, so they sat and rested every so often as they toured the garden. Melody didn't want to overtax his strength.

They held hands and talked a lot. He stole kisses from her. The attraction between them intensified.

They finally left and found a good Chinese buffet. Griz overate, but he'd lost weight while in captivity. Even though the thought made him think of himself as a zoo animal, it was an apt description. He needed to gain a few pounds, and healing his ankle kept burning his calories.

Griz enjoyed Melody's company. He told her about his life ranching and the mountains in Colorado.

She told him about college and her dream to start her clothing line. She was his dream. Melody was everything.

At six o'clock, they found the outlet shops. They stopped in a men's store, and Griz picked out some shirts in the style he preferred. He got measured, ordered several to be finished, and paid to have them delivered to Fox's address, along with a couple of good leather belts and two wide-brimmed stetson hats.

They promised he'd have it by tomorrow afternoon. Griz tipped well.

He stopped in several stores Melody liked and bought her several dresses, blouses, jeans, and shorts, and some new shoes and sandals. He even bought her a couple of pairs of sunglasses.

They passed a lingerie store. Melody blushed. Griz gave her a debit card and whispered the PIN. He left her there as he went in search of some good Levis.

He bought ten pairs in his size and was in a jewelry store when Melody texted him she'd finished. He asked her to wait there, and he would pick her up. Griz asked the jeweler to box up the necklace, bracelets, and earrings he liked and left to pick up Melody.

The backseat of the Hummer was full of purchases. Griz smiled, and Melody grinned. She gave him back his debit card and the receipt. At eight forty-five, they drove back to Fox's house. It was a perfect outing.

He wanted to kiss her again. But he had offered to dreamwalk and help with healing.

"Melody, I need to dreamwalk with Kallik at about ten. Will you be okay?"

"Do I need to leave the room? Will I disturb you if I stay and organize the chests and the closet for us?"

She wanted to go through the shopping bags. He could see her excitement.

"I won't be asleep, but I need you not to touch me. If you can do that and as long as there are no sudden loud noises, I would prefer it if you stayed. Text Melody's man to meet us in the driveway, and we'll get some help to drag this stuff inside."

They pulled into the driveway a little before nine-thirty. Melody's man waited for them. They got all the bags, but it took a few trips.

Griz left Melody, drove the Hummer back to Eli's, and met Ryker and Luke talking with another man in the driveway. Griz got down from the Hummer and walked toward the three men in the driveway.

He knew the other man. He seemed familiar somehow, although Griz couldn't seem to recall meeting him before.

"Dreamwalker. I see you got the boots I sent. Do they fit well?"

He must be Kallik. That was why he seemed familiar. He was the Kodiak bear from the dream.

"They do indeed. They're even in my style. Thank you. Do you still need help with the maned wolf?"

Griz clasped forearms with Kallik, Luke, and Ryker.

"I do. Will you assist us?" Kallik asked.

"It would be an honor. Will you review my dream for flaws?" Griz requested.

"I received your request. I will. Do you mind if I show the review to Eli in case she needs to assist another?" Kallik asked.

"Not at all. It is how we learn. Thank you for your help."

Griz respected the older dreamwalker. Kallik was powerful. Griz had never met a dreamwalker with the abilities Kallik had.

"Would you consider teaching another student?"

"Will you join the pack?" Kallik asked.

"I'm undecided."

Griz admitted the truth. It might be worth it to stay and learn the dream.

"I will teach you if you choose to stay," Kallik replied.

Kallik wouldn't waste his time teaching the one who left.

Griz handed the keys to the Hummer back to Ryker, thanking him for loaning it to him.

Luke asked Griz if he thought he might like to drive out to see Draoithe and survey the land tomorrow around four o'clock, maybe a bit earlier. Griz grinned.

He wanted to see it. He'd been thinking about it since he realized he lost his job in Colorado. Griz and Luke walked toward the dragon's house as Griz went back to Melody.

"You read my mind. Can Melody come?" Griz asked.

Luke grinned at him.

"Can't part with her, can you?"

Griz shook his head. Luke laughed.

"Javier and Andrei had the same problem. It will ease up once you bond with her. It won't go away, but you won't feel the need to orbit one another. I invited Isabell, Artie, and Fox to tag along. Javier will be there when we get there. Fox can look out for the ladies while we check out the land. Isabell can sketch Melody's ideas for a boutique and seamstress workspace. Artie needs to be with Fox, but Melody and Artie seem to understand one another. They're both submissives."

"Sounds good."

Luke was thoughtful. He still wanted Melody to feel at home, and he knew she was uncomfortable around the men. So he invited women to make sure Melody would be okay. Griz appreciated that.

Luke's people mattered to him. He wanted Griz and Melody to become part of the group. Griz liked the man.

"Meet at Eli's around three-thirty, and we'll travel together?"

Griz nodded and headed back to Melody as Luke went into the dragon's house. Griz needed to meditate.

CHAPTER SEVENTEEN

Team Player

G^{*riz*}

Griz settled into the chair in the room he shared with Melody. He closed his eyes and relaxed. She quietly put the purchases away and organized the space.

He'd warned her it might be several hours and reminded her not to touch him. She'd draw him to her if she did that. He narrowed his focus to a single point, then he stepped into the dream, a grizzly bear.

Griz stepped into Melody's barn. He liked the dream she'd built for herself. It had become his dream start. He wasn't as powerful as Kallik. Griz had his dream, but he had never built it. He didn't know how to draw another into it, as Kallik could do.

He had the strength to help fix other dreams, and he could temporarily seize control of another's dream. He'd stumbled over that seeking Melody.

His great teacher had lost his mate before Griz could learn the skills Kallik had. His teacher faded afterward. Griz hadn't known of another dreamwalker willing to teach. So he'd simply paused that part of his life.

He moved through the dream, seeking Kallik. He found the Kodiak bear in the forest where they first met. Kallik had created a veritable paradise. It was peaceful.

When he found Kallik, Eli was with him. The fierce little tiger lay in a patch of sun in the dappled forest. She, too, enjoyed the sanctuary of Kallik's dreamscape.

Griz greeted the other two dreamwalkers. Eli rose and circled him. Here, even though she was Kallik's pack alpha female, Kallik held the authority. Kallik addressed him.

Griz, I think perhaps we should review your dream first. If you're unwell, I wouldn't wish to compromise you further by bringing you into the dreamwalk with the maned wolf. Will you give control of the dream to me? Kallik asked.

Kallik could just take control if he chose, but the big Kodiak bear preferred a gentler method. Griz wondered if a light touch was an inherent trait in bears.

Bear shifters were big and usually strong. Just because a man had strength didn't mean he needed to use it forcefully. Griz took great care with delicate things to avoid damaging them. Kallik was the same.

Yes. Please show me if there is anything amiss.

Do you have reason to believe there would be an issue?

Kallik wanted to know the root cause behind Griz's request for a review.

Injected with drugs meant as a cure or an antidote for my bear shifter 'affliction', I couldn't control the shift for weeks. When Smoke reached for Melody, I lost control and shifted, but it felt different. I'd like to know if I'll be able to keep control of my magic in the future. It's unsettling.

Griz admitted the truth about what had happened without guilt or shame. He hadn't been in control of what happened to him. He needed to know if it was permanent or would continue to short-circuit his magic.

I think I see. I believe I know what we seek. Eli, we'll walk into Griz's dream. When we step into his dream, I'll take control of it. I need you to look for one thing out of place in the scene. It is something small, but significant.

Griz, I want you to look at your dream as well. You may see nothing wrong, but maybe you'll know it right away. I'll have control of it so if either of you sees anything which seems wrong, let me know. I would study it before we correct it so I can recognize it later. Shall we go?

The three of them walked shoulder to shoulder into Griz's dreamscape. Griz frowned.

He was in Melody's barn. How did that happen? They were to go to Griz's dream, not to Melody's.

Kallik, there's been a mistake. We've entered Melody's dream. This is her barn where her owl roosts. I've come here often recently, but it's her dream, not mine.

No, there is no mistake. This is your dream. I can feel Melody's dream, faded but near. She's awake. Eli, can you bring forth a mirror? Kallik asked.

Yes, I see what you mean.

Eli closed her eyes and concentrated. A mirror appeared before them.

Griz, look at yourself. Do you see the difference? Kallik asked.

Griz studied himself in the mirror. He saw a grizzly bear. Was it himself?

He moved, and the image in the mirror moved. It was himself, but not as he had once been.

His paws were black where they'd been brown once. His fur was silver-streaked. He hadn't been so grizzled before. Someone pierced his bear's ears and threaded a loop of rawhide through the holes.

Dangling on the loop of rawhide were soft, long flight feathers. They were snow white with golden brown flecks. The tips were red, dipped in blood. The hollow shafts were the palest yellow, filled, and stained with tears. They were Melody's feathers.

It's me, but I'm changed. Why? It's not my dream that is wrong, but myself that is different.

Melody came to us to help you. She said you wouldn't stop talking to her in her mind. Perhaps Luke misunderstood. He thought she described your dreamtalk to her. But you had left your dream to go to hers because you were dying. She stole your awareness from you, as birds do with their mates. You fell into her, and she kept you. She gave you back to yourself when we brought you here. But not before you were strong enough to go back.

Eli carefully explained the events he had slept through.

She called you back in the dream, the night that we healed Artie. Your mate called you, and you fled the dream to go to her. She sent you back to yourself then. Melody changed you, changed your dream. She gave you her anger over what happened to you, her frustration at her inability to help you, and the softness of her love for her mate. She claimed your dream self and marked you as hers. Her dream became your dream. Do you see it? Kallik asked.

Yes, I see it. I had to learn to shift to this version of myself. The old version was no longer who I am. I used the anger she gave me to shift into this form. That's why the shift felt strange.

Griz spoke as he thought it out.

Melody had saved his bear. She'd taken his mind and kept it.

He'd wanted to fade. He'd wanted an end to the torment. Griz remembered.

He thought for a moment and shifted in the dream to his human form and then back to his bear immediately. Griz didn't trace in the light. He traced in the flame, the way Melody had when she shifted into her owl.

Griz, I think your dream is correct. It's you who has altered. I believe it to be a permanent change.

Kallik stated the truth.

91

Thank you for reviewing my dream. We have a hard time correcting our own dreams. You have my gratitude and respect.

Griz appreciated Kallik. The old dreamwalker was both knowledgeable and powerful.

Griz, will you consider staying here at Draoithe? Luke spoke the truth when he admitted wanting you for a Ruiri. Others feel the strength of your magic as well. None would be happy to see you go.

Eli asked Griz to stay with the power of the alpha clear at her request. She was serious. She wanted him to join the pack. Eli would keep him at Draoithe as an asset to their group.

Griz had never been much of a team player.

CHAPTER EIGHTEEN

Griz Sat

G^{riz}

*Griz, your potential to surpass even my ability in the dream
is enormous. You have already done things you lacked skills in. You
requested a teacher, but I would offer mutual sharing if you stayed.
We could explore what you've done with the dream. I would add my
encouragement to my alpha's plea.*

Kallik was honest about his reasons for wishing Griz would join
the pack. Kallik's offer to help him learn and expand his skill as a
dreamwalker appealed to Griz. It was a temptation.

*I'll seriously consider it. Thank you for your offer. Now, I believe there
is a maned wolf who requires our help?*

May I control the dream? Kallik requested.

Both Griz and Eli agreed. Kallik had more skill than either of them.
They stepped shoulder to shoulder into the maned wolf's dream.

When they arrived, Kallik allowed Eli to speak first. Eli introduced
them to Raven. She was a pretty, but fearful, maned wolf.

Griz knew her as another submissive immediately. Kallik took control of her dream and blocked any exit.

Eli took the lead and began the conversation with Raven about her warped dream. As Eli guided Raven to correct things in her dream and stretch the shifter magic in her mind, Kallik and Griz corrected other parts of her dream. It would save Raven's strength and allow her to focus on things only she would view as incorrect.

It wasn't as long or involved as correcting Artie's dream. Raven had been a maned wolf for only a couple of weeks. Griz was much stronger than he'd ever been in the dream.

He knew time passed differently in the dream, but he also knew it went well. Raven would be safe.

When they finished and Raven had put the final touches on her dream by barking at a stone, she didn't like until it changed size and shape, Kallik addressed Raven.

You did a good job, little one. The three of us need to step out of your dream. You must promise to keep it this way. Do not allow it to revert to what it was. Will you do it?

Raven nodded. She was shy with the big Kodiak bear, but her dreamscape pleased her.

When we leave, you need to wake and eat food, drink water, then get rest. You mustn't touch any magic for two weeks. I need you to tell Ash. He must protect you from all the magic for two weeks. Do not forget to tell him. It's important.

Eat, drink, rest, and do no magic for two weeks. I can do it.

Raven repeated his instructions.

No shifting. Do you understand? Kallik asked.

I don't even know how to shift.

Wait to learn how. You don't need to shift until the magic settles. In about two weeks, you'll have to shift. The magic will force it; wait until it happens before you touch any magic. That will be how you know it's safe for you. Okay, little one?

Kallik spoke kindly to the maned wolf.

Thank you all. It was kind of you to help me.

The three dreamwalkers assured her it was their pleasure to help. Kallik released Raven's dream, and the three dreamwalkers stepped shoulder to shoulder out of Raven's dream and back to Kallik's dream.

You did well, Eli. Raven should be fine. Tell Luke he will have his bartender.

With your permission, dreamwalker, I'm tired. Griz, thank you for your help. I'll know you in the waking world.

Kallik nodded his permission to his student. Eli winked out of the dream.

Thank you again for reviewing my dream. It has given me much to ponder. I have a new insight.

Griz spoke to Kallik once Eli left.

Griz had questions he hoped Melody would help him answer. He wished to return to her.

Thank you for your help with the maned wolf. The review of your dream was the most interesting review I've ever taken part in. It has left me with questions to ponder about the power of the dream. If I can be of help in the future, do not hesitate to call me. I would know you if you're willing to stay and share it.

Kallik admitted his curiosity.

The offer is tempting. I will know you in the waking world.

Griz nodded and stepped back to his dream.

The mirror was still in his barn. Griz studied himself. It didn't upset him. He was still a large grizzly bear.

Griz was glad his mate was a bird shifter. He would've died had she not been. He owed her a far larger debt of gratitude than he'd previously understood.

Griz realized he'd built his barn and that struck him hard. He'd copied Melody's, but he'd built his dream and called Melody to it. He was in his barn.

Kallik was right. He had a lot more strength than he'd known. Was it because of Melody? Or had he always had it and not been skilled enough to use it?

He missed Melody. It was past the time to depart from the dream and find something to eat. He wanted to hold his mate in his arms and thank her for saving him. Griz winked out of the dream.

He sat in the chair. He blinked in the dim light. It was after midnight, but not as late as he'd feared it would be.

Melody had reorganized the space around him and put all of their purchases away. She studied something on her phone. The blue glow of the screen illuminated her face.

She was beautiful. Her long white hair streaked with dark blonde strands reflected the blue glow into the room.

Her scent of *gardenia* filled the room. He breathed it in. Griz's world was right as long as his snowy owl was in it. He needed her.

"Melody?" Griz said.

Melody looked up at him and smiled.

"I hoped you'd be back soon. Were you successful?"

"Yes, the rest is up to Raven. If she follows Kallik's instructions, she should be fine."

Griz smiled at Melody.

"I have a bear-sized appetite. Shall we go to the kitchen and see if there's anything to eat?"

Melody laughed. Her laugh was soft and light. Griz liked it. He could hear her laughter forever. He had to make her laugh more. Her happiness and joy meant everything to him.

"Yeah, I wouldn't want you to waste away on me."

She teased him shyly.

Griz rose and stretched. They went in search of food. When they got to the kitchen, it didn't surprise Griz to find Nadine sipping tea with Andrei, Ryker, and a pretty black-haired lady. She must be the panther.

Ryker introduced Lily to Griz, and he saw why Ryker liked her. She was beautiful in a catlike fashion. She was no Melody, but she had an open, kind expression.

Nadine asked if Griz was hungry.

"Yes ma'am. I'm starving. The dreamwalk took a lot out of me," Griz said.

"Fox left you a plate in the fridge with instructions to heat it in the microwave in sections with the paper towels over it," Nadine said.

"Thanks, sit Griz. I'll get it for you." Melody said.

Griz looked at Melody. She'd helped him so much, and she still helped him. He preferred to do things for himself, but it felt good when she took care of him. Her kindness helped him heal faster.

"Thank you, Melody. I appreciate it."

Griz sat as she had instructed him.

CHAPTER NINETEEN

The Entire Story

Griz

"Were you successful in helping the maned wolf?" Andrei asked.

"Yes. Raven should be fine, as long as she avoids any magic for a couple of weeks. It was a good dreamwalk."

Griz shared with the others at the table. It felt good to sit down at the table with them. He wasn't a team player, but he did like the company at meals.

"Have you got any plans for tomorrow?" Andrei asked.

"Luke invited Melody and me out to see the land tomorrow afternoon. I admit I'm curious to see it."

Melody served Griz two heaping plates of fried fish, hush puppies, fries, and coleslaw. Griz's mouth watered. He liked fish. Fox seasoned the fish perfectly.

He could seriously get spoiled eating at Draoithe. He vowed never to mention the fox's guilty pleasure of playing with his food if it always tasted so good.

"It's ninety-five acres of near-pristine wild land. There are two small lakes, and Javier has done a good job overseeing all the construction. There's no mess. He's even laid out plans for creating horse trails through the land to avoid damaging the environment with vehicles. You'll like the log cabin, I think. The windows are quite nice. We have almost completed the stable now. Fox wants to take a trip in a few weeks to check out some more horses. Mihaela is excited. She wants to invest in some good mares for pleasure riding," Andrei said.

"Luke mentioned something about building a barn and running cattle on the land and starting an organic vegetable farming outfit for the restaurant. Are you staying to help with that? The restaurant would be so much more profitable if we didn't have to outsource all of our food supplies." Lily asked.

"I have a lot to consider. I can't lie and say I'm not intrigued, but I had never thought to join a pack. There are some business affairs I have to handle in Colorado. Melody would be happier here, though. I'll see this land and think about it further," Griz said.

"Well, I hope you stay. You could contribute to Draoithe. I'm a panther, and it's strange to hear me say it. But it feels good to work toward common goals with people who appreciate your skill and expertise. Panthers are usually solitary, but no one steps on my toes here. It's a good place to be," Lily said.

"I have to agree with Lily. I'm a Philippine eagle. Solitary apex predators rarely like to share territory, but I found a good niche here. I can fly free at Draoithe. Luke even considered my insomnia when he offered me the job. He left my working hours up to me. The pay didn't change when I had to hunt for Andrei, because he was on house arrest for drinking a man dry and getting drunk from it. Andrei's pay didn't change when he raided a warehouse to get eight people out of captivity, either. The pack comes first." Nadine said.

"I can protect Nadine better here. She is everything. The pack works for all of us and helps us accomplish our goals. It's a haven for magical misfits and the unwanted of the immortal world. I couldn't always protect Nadine if we lived in the Domhain. Elliot's people stalked her in Seattle. Here, I have support from my friends whom I also support," Andrei said.

"I served with Luke in the military. He was the best. Luke always had well thought out plans. Every man volunteered for missions he led because he didn't lose men. His people mattered to him. He always heard counsel before giving orders. I would follow the colonel into Hell. If he said he needed a man to go, I'm his man. You couldn't ask for a better commander."

Ryker endorsed Draoithe from the top down.

"What's the deal with Javier and the dripping fire?" Griz asked. He had to know how that worked.

"Javier was friends with Luke and worked for Luke as a human. When Elliot sent someone looking for Luke, they attacked Eli instead. Javier defended her but got cut up badly. The man broke a shifter's jaw and arm before the shifter got the better of him. Luke had to turn Javier to save his friend. Fox fled California after rescuing Isabell from one of Elliot's warehouses there. It traumatized Isabell. Javier sheltered her and fell for her instantly. Isabell is a phoenix, and she controls the frozen flame. She's a first-order shifter. She turned her mate into a keeper of the flames, but he'd become a direwolf only a week before. He's half direwolf and half keeper, but he has full ability in both magics."

Andrei explained.

"There's a lot of magic here. Why is that?" Griz asked.

"None of us knows, but the current theory is: we are the magic's answer to the imbalance Elliot's causing in the dream. The magic here is all balanced and extremely powerful. Some have multiple magics. The magic seems to call lifemates as well. Bonded lifemates all have enhanced gifts. Bonded men can wield the Druid magic as well."

Ryker explained.

"It also seems to keep attracting people with skills Draoithe can use. Like I'm a chef. Ryker is a mechanic. Andrei and Nadine are IT Specialists. Kallik is a stable master. Mihaela is the event planner. Isabell is a talented artist. We have a few friendly wagers on the women Luke rescued from those warehouses. Eli has the Inner Circle interviewing them and making job offers."

Lily grinned.

"I heard the maned wolf, Raven, has agreed to be the bar manager. She negotiated for Ash to remain assigned to her and demanded he live with her. Fox cried from laughing at that one when he came to help with the data entry this afternoon."

Nadine chuckled.

"Griz, you'd fit in here. Give it a serious thought. Nadine, will you fly with me?"

Andrei asked his consort after Griz nodded.

"Oh, yes. Let's go. We'll see y'all later."

Andrei and Nadine rose and left to fly.

"I'm tired. Are you ready, Melody? Lily, it was a pleasure to meet you. Ryker."

Griz nodded goodnight as he and Melody made their way back to their room.

"Melody, can we talk for a minute? I need to ask you some things."

Griz asked after the door closed behind them. He took both of her tiny hands in his big ones as he stood before her. She was beyond beautiful. No woman had ever held him so enraptured.

"Sure, Griz. What do you need to know?"

Melody wanted to please him and help him. She was the best mate he could've imagined. He didn't deserve her, but he wouldn't give her up.

"When I was a captive, Luke suggested I dreamtalked to you. Can you tell me about that? I think you have the information I need. Do you recall what I said, or how we communicated? My memory is fuzzy or blank in places. I need to puzzle out what happened to me."

Griz explained to her.

"At first, you came to my barn, but then you asked me who I was. I got scared and woke up. You didn't hurt me, even though you were fearsome. I thought you liked me. I liked you. The next night, we talked in the dream. Later you called me from flying, and then I was in the barn. I answered you when you called. After that, every time I slept, I found you in the dream. When you weren't there anymore, I grew fearful. I cried for you. You were nice to me. I missed my friend."

Melody had cried for losing his company in the dream. He mattered to her, but it hurt him she'd been upset. Nothing had worked as he'd wanted. He would've never intentionally caused her any harm.

"The next time you called to me in the dream, I went to you, but you were in a cage, battered and bloody. My owl shrieked in outrage. I tried to comfort you. I could only just reach you with the tips of my flight feathers, but they came away stained with your blood. My heart ached for the damage which had been done. You recognized me, but delirious with pain, you fell into me, seeking relief. I flew away with you, but you still hurt."

She shook her head sadly.

"You begged me for help. I hurt for you. I knew I had to help you. You were dying. I went to some bears I'd met in California, and they sent me here. I explained as best as I could to Luke and the others, but I was nervous. Luke agreed to help me and asked me to stay so I wouldn't accidentally endanger you."

Melody told him the entire story.

CHAPTER TWENTY
Sleep Took Him

G^{riz}

Kallik had been right. Griz had lost himself in his owl, but she'd saved him. She'd taken his awareness. She'd changed him. Melody took his suffering.

Had being mesmerized so long erased some of his memory? Or had the drugs and seizures done that?

"You mesmerized me on purpose, didn't you?"

"Yes, and no. I wanted to take your fear away and make you calm. I never tried it on a predator before. It worked, sort of. Your body relaxed. Everything slowed down. You still hurt, but it slowed the bleeding. You didn't shake as much. When you fell into me, it felt right, so I took you. I didn't understand until Isabell explained it to me."

She feared his anger with her. He'd fallen into her, and she'd sent his body into hibernation. Melody had saved his life. She'd given him time to heal and eased his suffering.

"You saved my life. I wanted it to stop, to fade. The pain was too great. I think you sent me into hibernation. When you sleepwalked to me, you

104

touched me when you lay down next to me. You sent me back then. I woke up. My body had been healing for a while by that point. I hurt, but it was tolerable. You were there with me, asleep beside me. I thought it was a beautiful dream, but it was you."

"How did I look when I shifted this morning? Was I different from when you first saw me?"

He had to know if he looked in the waking world as he did in the dream.

"You were different. Your feet were blacker, and you have pierced ears with feathers threaded on loops of rawhide. They are white feathers with golden brown flecks, and the shafts are pale yellow. The tips are dark red. Your fur has more silver streaks in it and is more grizzled-looking. Before you were browner. No piercings. You are much bigger than I'd originally thought you would be."

He was her grizzly bear. Griz looked as she wanted her bear to look. He knew it was true when he saw her shy smile as she described him.

It excited her to think of how he looked. Her eyes brightened with the memory. Her face flushed.

Griz remained the same as he'd been before as a man. She hadn't altered him to suit her fancy. She'd never seen him as a man. It was the bear she'd rescued. It was the dreamwalker she wanted.

That she liked the way he looked like a man was icing on the cake. She wanted Griz in all his forms. She'd even given him enough of her righteous anger to relearn how to shift.

Griz groaned as he realized he needed to apologize to Smoke. The magic and the side effects of all the drugs had taken him for a ride. Smoke hadn't deserved his wrath.

"Are you okay, Griz?"

"I'm better than I've ever been, but I owe Smoke an apology. The magic took me. He was a harmless catalyst. It was all you, Melody. You saved me, but I was too weak. Your shifter magic burned me in the flames of your thoughts in the dream. It changed me. I had to learn how to become the new version you wanted me to be. Everything will be good. I know what happened to me now. Thank-you."

Griz smiled at her.

"I'm indebted to you. You did far more than help me. I'll never be the same, but I've never been happier."

She looked into his eyes.

Griz fell. It wasn't as slow as it had been before. It was hard and fast. Griz fell deep. He wanted to drown in his snowy owl.

He kissed her then. Griz kissed her hard with all the passion his new understanding had lent to him. He kissed her fiercely. He was a bear.

She was his mate. She desired him. The scent of *gardenia* swirled around him, dragging him further into her.

Melody kissed him back, and he lost control. His desire for his mate took him. Griz groaned into the kiss, bent, and picked her up by slipping his arm beneath her knees. He set her gently on the bed and followed her down, covering her slight frame with his larger one. He kissed her with authority.

She moaned and writhed against him, rubbing herself wantonly against his erection. He had to have her. He needed to take his mate for his own.

He rumbled at her clothes being in the way of him, feeling her skin next to his. He ripped her blouse off and used a claw to slice open her bra. His mouth fell on her nipple when he saw her breasts.

They fit in the palm of his hand. He squeezed the delicate globes and exulted in her warble of pleasure.

He reached down and unbuttoned her pants, and she lifted her hips so he could remove them along with her panties. When she lay naked on the bed, he looked her over. She blushed prettily.

"So sexy. I have to have you, please. May I take you for mine? I'll always protect you and provide for you. Will you take your bear as your mate?"

"Take me. Promise not to look away."

"I'll never look away. Will you drink from me?"

Her head shifted, and before he could move, she had sliced his neck open. She'd marked him. She shifted and drank him down.

He bit into her soft throat to drink from her as well. She tasted divine. Griz got high on her blood. He smiled as he thought he might float away.

He felt her hands on his pants, unbuttoning them as he ripped off his shirt. When his cock sprang free, she immediately grabbed it and licked it like a popsicle.

Griz groaned in pleasure so loud the windows rattled. He didn't care. He would be Melody's bear.

He couldn't stand her teasing him, not when he wanted her so badly. He pushed her back onto the bed and knelt between her legs. His fingers slipped between her folds.

She was wet, and it made his cock throb. He tasted the sweetness of her as he licked her honey off of his fingers.

"Look at me, my snowy owl. I'm going to pleasure you until you scream my name. Do not look away from me. I intend to claim you as mine."

He slid into her then, filling her. Griz was home.

He lifted her hips and pressed his hard cock into her center. He reached down, lightly and skillfully, stroking her clit with the same rhythm as he used his cock to slide into her.

He rocked into her. It was like liquid fire racing through his veins. He needed to stroke her with every inch of his member.

Deep was the only way. He touched her center. Griz fell into her eyes. He never wanted to leave. The intensity was unbelievable.

Watching her pleasure cross her face as he gazed into her soul set his soul ablaze for her. She was the sexiest woman he'd ever known. Nothing in his long life had ever prepared him for how desperate he was to take this one woman as his bonded mate.

Melody screamed his name, and the erotic echo of his name falling from her lips made him want to hear it again. He stopped stroking her clit and gently squeezed her nipples. He rocked her faster.

The magic wanted their energy. Griz didn't look away from her. He stroked her harder. She moaned in ecstasy as she watched him drowning in the pleasure of being one with her. They gave the magic the energy it desired.

Griz leaned into her, and her hands raked across his back as she begged him to give himself to her. He belonged to her. She had remade him as her bear. He wanted no other.

Melody ruined him for other women, and he wallowed in his ruination. No other woman would ever satisfy him as she did.

He felt her climax rising. She would cum for him hard and long. He would force her to clench him so hard it would hurt.

Griz wanted it. He stroked her so hard and fast the bed moved over the floor with their lovemaking.

"Cum for me now. I'm going to follow you. It's too tight. Too good."

She screamed his name again. The light bulb in the lamp shattered. He pounded into her harder still, drawing her pleasure out as she came again. Her sheath walls tightened up around his shaft, squeezing him without mercy.

Griz roared her name at his release. The force of their lovemaking hit him hard, and the link opened in his mind, flooding him with her pleasure. The magic burned their souls together, searing his heart, so he cried out at the pain.

He almost didn't mark it when her beak sliced his vein open again. He left his member buried inside her when he felt her pull his blood into her body.

Griz rumbled as he came again, so hard it stung. He throbbed as he bit her and drank from her. She climaxed again, clenching around him as he drank from her. She was too much.

His soul burned. The flame in his mind seared into him. His heart squeezed tight. He felt her emotions in his mind.

She floated in bliss. His mate felt satisfied. Griz waited until he caught his breath and rolled to one side to pull her close to him.

Griz, that was fierce. I'm spent, but my mind wants you again. How is that even possible?

I don't know. I feel the same way. Nothing has ever been so intense. I'm in awe. I need sleep, or I swear I would oblige you immediately.

We have to fix things tomorrow. I think we need a heavier bed.

I'll build us one. Otherwise, we may break them.

I'm almost certain we broke the window. Thank you, Griz. That was amazing.

I'm lost to you, Melody, completely lost. I'm the bear you made me.

I need you. I'm not strong enough on my own. Be always mine and mine alone. I need to feel you get lost in me. Fall into me.

Forever.

Griz held his mate tight. He had his owl. No one would take her from him, and he would see to it she always flew free. Melody was everything. Sleep took him.

CHAPTER TWENTY-ONE
Better Than Any Magic

M *elody*

The morning had flown by. Breakfast and talking with Artie and Isabell while Isabell painted had been fun. Griz had left her to seek the dragon, Smoke, and apologize to him. Isabell and Artie had both laughed when they teased her about needing a new light bulb and a window in her room.

"So you took your mate. Are you happy?"

Isabell smiled while she painted.

"Yes, Griz is everything. I needed his strength, and he gave it to me. I just hope he stays here because I fear life will be hard for him since he suffered. Although he is independent, there is definitely room for improvement in terms of his care. Griz could achieve more if he were to stay. He's powerful. I can feel it, and he'd like to learn more. Kallik offered to explore the dream with him if he stayed," Melody admitted.

"He should stay. He's a farmer, a rancher. We need his expertise. What would it take to convince him?" Artie asked.

"The outdoors speak to him. Luke invited us to see the land. Maybe that will be enough."

Melody was hopeful.

Griz could be stubborn. He'd made it plain he believed there were things which were right and wrong. Griz needed to protect and provide for his mate. He'd done so.

He wasn't the man to be told what to do. Neither was he the man who needed to be told. His character refused questioning.

He had a keen sense of honor. It was why he'd gone in search of Smoke. Griz felt he had to right a wrong.

He had the patience to wait until he had all the information before he acted. He would most certainly handle a situation instantly if he needed to do so.

Griz was a real man with old-fashioned ideas about how he should behave, but it was a good way for a man as large as he was to be.

"If you choose to stay, he won't leave. He's looking at it all with your desire to stay with us as a deciding factor for him. He wants you to be happy, and your comfort matters more to him than the money or business he has elsewhere. I believe Draoithe will meet his requirements. Plus, Luke's talented at making offers which no one refuses."

Isabell suggested Griz might stay. It made Melody more hopeful to hear Isabell explain it. She wanted to stay.

"Luke knows what he's doing. Duncan and I have never been part of a pack before we came. For four hundred years, we traveled the world and researched magic and immortals. When we met Luke, Duncan told me he was special. Luke was still in the military then. He hadn't been a direwolf for long. For a long time, Duncan searched for anyone worthy of his loyalty. Luke was worthy. Griz will learn that too."

Artie smiled. Melody liked Artie. Artie treated her with kindness from the start. She and Fox had seemed like the easiest of the pack to approach when she arrived. Fox was a powerful alpha, but his aura didn't press on her as Luke's and Javier's did.

His magic was quieter, more subtle. Artie was submissive to Fox, who was her alpha. She had powerful magic too, but it was purely defensive.

Isabell was a bird shifter like Melody, but she was a first-order shifter. As a phoenix, she commanded the phoenix fire. She was an alpha, but her alpha presence echoed Fox's a little, in that it wasn't overt.

Isabell had explained a lot about the unique abilities of bird shifters to Melody. Melody hadn't been completely clueless.

Melody's grandmother had been a great grey owl, but her mother hadn't inherited the gene. On her twenty-fifth birthday, her grandmother called to invite her out for coffee. Melody hadn't seen her in years.

When she got to the coffee shop, a young woman about her age waved at her. It was her grandmother, but she'd never aged.

Her grandmother had explained to Melody about being a shifter. Melody remembered her relief at finding her. It had kept her from thinking she was crazy, but it hadn't helped her life greatly.

She'd learned enough to know about shifters, immortality, and mates. The unique ability to allow their mate to fall into them, her grandmother had either not known or forgotten to share.

Owls are lone apex predators mostly until they find a mate. Her grandmother hadn't found her mate when Melody spoke with her last.

"Thank you, Artie. I hope you're right. Hey, can you guys explain something to me? How do you all have so many magics?"

Melody was just an owl, but no one else at Draoithe was just anything, except maybe Isabell.

"I have nothing but the magic of a phoenix shifter. I was born with it as you were born an owl shifter. Phoenixes just wield their flame overtly. We are offensive magic wielders, whereas you are a defensive magic wielder," Isabell explained.

"I turned into an arctic fox, but I learned white magic afterward. I can't show you now because I have to wait about ten more days until my magic heals," Artie explained.

"I was born human, with no magic at all."

"The vampires are weaker than shifters, with peculiar sensitivities to light and unable to ingest solid food. All the vampires here possess the magic of Volos. They gain added abilities. There are others with elemental powers, and even a sorceress and a Nephilim among us now. Some turned, some born. Those who take a mate have added gifts. Eli can dreamwalk, but only since she mated with Luke. He can dreamtalk. All the vampires and their mates can teleport if they are also consorts." Isabell said.

"Wait, what do you mean added gifts?" Melody asked.

"When a shifter bonds with their mate, the magic combines as it fuses their souls. The alpha usually gains power. The submissive usually gains a new attribute," Artie said.

"I don't think I gained anything new. Should I feel different?" Melody frowned.

"No, you should feel the same. In my case, I'm now more powerful. Javier received the phoenix flame," Isabell said.

"I'm not the alpha," Melody said.

"Neither am I, not with Javier, but as a first-order shifter, my magic was greater than his. He hadn't been a direwolf shifter for a week when my phoenix claimed her mate, so the magic saw him as the weaker one of us," Isabell said.

"Does it manifest immediately?" Melody asked.

"I think it does, but some shifters have to figure out what it is. For me, it was telekinesis. I can move things with my thoughts, but it was an accident that I discovered it," Artie explained.

"Griz is more powerful. I felt it at breakfast," Isabell said.

"I must figure it out then, because I don't know of anything other than the telepathy. That's different," Melody said.

"It'll come to you. Just wait."

"Artie, you look like you just ate the gingerbread man. What gives?" Isabell asked.

"The first time I used telekinesis was on Duncan," Artie answered.

"Is this going to be a clean story?" Isabell laughed.

"I never kiss and tell," Artie said.

They all laughed.

"So what happened?" Melody asked.

"Duncan was teaching me to read. I'd gotten frustrated, and my temper at my inability to decipher the cursed letters got the better of me. I flung the book away from us without touching it. It hit the wall with a satisfying thump, but it was one of Duncan's books. I broke the spine on it. That man loves books. Sadness overwhelmed him. Shock washed over me. We worked on telekinetic manipulation for months after, so I had control. Duncan wanted no more of his books destroyed. Looking back now, it was rather comical, but it was scary when it manifested."

Artie shared her story.

"Sometimes the magical gifts are more personal. I can sift through Javier's memories. Sometimes it's cool. I have seen him as a boy, learning to drive, and smoking his first joint. Sometimes it's not cool. He has memories of being with other women, being in fights, and losing at love, too. They all tell the story of who he is to me from his unique perspective. I like it, but it wouldn't be useful to anyone but me," Isabell explained.

"I see what you mean. It doesn't matter to me if I have no special magical talent. I have Griz, and he's everything."

Melody smiled. She had Griz, and he was better than any magic there could be.

Chapter Twenty-Two

Apologize

M^{elody}

"Let's break for some lunch, shall we? It's almost one o'clock. Ryker's pupils will have to wait."

Isabell spoke of the eyes she painted.

"How about sandwiches? We have bread and lunch meats. I thought I saw some tortilla chips and salsa too," Artie said.

"Are you sure you don't want soup?"

Isabell gave Melody a wink.

"I might throw up. Duncan thinks I'm sick, so he keeps making me eat soup. I'm not sick."

"I think sandwiches sound good. No soup for me, either."

Artie smiled conspiratorially with Melody.

"Well, don't tell Fox I didn't make you eat soup."

Isabell smiled as she cleaned her brushes.

Melody laughed. The two women were good people. They had been friends for a long time, but they had made her feel welcome. She liked them. Nadine and Lily had been kind to her as well.

Eli was powerful. She, too, had been nice to her. Melody didn't know Mihaela, but the way Nadine and Lily had spoken of her made it seem as if she was as interesting as the others were. If Griz wanted to stay, Melody felt as if Draoithe could be home.

The three of them sat down to lunch when Eli came in and joined them. She was doing a two-week-long summer reading program for the advanced academic program half days in the morning for two weeks.

"How were your classes?" Isabell asked.

Eli made herself a sandwich to join them.

"It went well. Today, we went over the required reading list for the advanced courses, and then I gave them access to all the social studies writing rubrics. We took a tour of the library and the writing center. Next year's freshmen will take some college-level courses. Tomorrow, it will bore because they have to take a test for entrance into dual credit classes," Eli said.

"Melody, you look rested today. Have you given any more thought to staying with us here at Draoithe?" Eli asked.

"I think I want to stay, but I'm waiting to see what Griz wants. I want him more, but Luke's offer is more than tempting to me," Melody said.

Eli studied Melody for a minute, then smiled.

"You took him as your mate. Birds don't waste time at all."

Melody blushed. It hadn't seemed fast to her. She had known Griz in the dream before. Meeting him in real life only confirmed her feelings for him.

She wasn't about to give him the chance to change his mind. He was hers. Isabell patted her hand.

"It's okay. Cats and dogs don't understand, because their mates can't get as lost in them as ours can. It feels too good. You can only do it with your lifemate. I certainly wouldn't give that up. The flame of bird magic drives you. The only reason Nadine held out so long was because

Andrei wouldn't court her without Luke's permission, and eagles ritualize everything," Isabell said.

Melody hadn't planned on bonding with Griz. It just sort of happened. She wasn't sorry. She had followed her owl's instincts and claimed him.

It was simple. Isabell was right. The magic had been in control, but they both wanted it.

Melody was still in awe of how good being with Griz had been. He made her think every clumsy encounter she'd ever had before him had been a waste of time and energy.

"Nevermind the fact Javier and Isabell both seem to take crazy risks and almost killed one another with it."

Eli smiled impishly at Isabell.

"Javier lost consciousness, and when he woke up, he was drunk with too much magic for four days before it finally soaked in."

Artie laughed.

"I never heard him complain about it."

Isabell crossed her arms and huffed. They all laughed.

Luke and Fox walked in to join them. They'd been discussing some intelligence, Andrei discovered. Artie told them earlier. She knew little about it. Isabell had paled but steadied herself later.

"What's making all of you laugh?" Fox asked.

"We were teasing Melody about taking her mate, and the conversation turned to the story of how Javier got drunk for four days with a phoenix," Eli said.

"You'll never let him live one down, will you?"

Luke grinned.

"I told them he wasn't complaining about it. Besides, he's the best-looking keeper of the flames ever," Isabell said.

"You only say that because he's your keeper of the flames."

Fox teased Isabell.

"Maybe."

Isabel grinned. They all laughed again.

"Griz is an honorable man. I'm glad you came to us for help. He needed his mate. Congratulations. Where is he?" Luke asked.

Fox made more sandwiches, stacked them up on a plate, and sat down to share them with his alpha as Luke had served two glasses of iced tea for them.

"He left to find Smoke to apologize to him. I was the reason he couldn't shift properly, and he feels guilty," Melody said.

"I'm sorry. I'm not following. Can you start from the beginning of the story?" Fox asked.

He'd risen and collected a pen and a notebook.

"Yes, please. I think we all want to hear this story," Artie said.

"Well, as far as I understand it, it's wrapped up in the fact I'm a bird shifter, and he's a dreamwalker. I told you how he was dreamwalking with me, and I thought he liked me. Then he started calling me to the dream to see me. Then he disappeared, right?" Melody asked.

Luke nodded.

"When he called me to the warehouse, he was dying. I didn't know what I was doing, but he recognized me in the dream. He was hurting, so I tried to mesmerize him as I would do with prey. He got still, and his heart rate slowed way down. Griz said he thinks I sent him into hibernation."

"You may have saved his life. No wonder he was so unresponsive when we found him," Luke said.

"Well, it gets worse. When I talked with Isabell later, I discovered he fell into me. I know it was in the dream, but somehow, I kept his awareness and flew off with it. I brought him here with me in my head. He didn't dream talk to me. He was in my head," Melody said.

"Wait, how did he get back to himself, then?" Fox asked.

"When he got here, I found him again while I was asleep. He was back in the barn. He was safe. I wanted to see him again, and when I touched him in the dream, he looked at me. I had my bear. Griz says I must have touched him in the waking world when I lay down. He remembers waking up, thinking he was still dreaming, when he found me in bed next to him. Somehow, I changed him in the dream. His bear is different now."

Melody frowned. She still didn't understand how it could happen.

"What do you mean, you changed him? How?" Artie asked.

"I don't know how I did it. He was mostly brown with a bit of silver tipping on his fur when I first saw him in the dream. After I flew away with him, the way he looked changed. His feet got singed by the flames. They're black now. He's streaked with silver and far more grizzling of his fur than he once had. His ears have piercings now, and he wears my flight feathers on rawhide thongs looped through them. The feathers had red tips from my anger, and the shafts are pale yellow from the tears of my frustration."

Melody's voice faded away in a whisper toward the end. The tale seemed incredulous, even though she'd lived it.

"You claimed a dreamwalker as your mate in the dream and marked him as yours?"

Fox whistled softly.

"Yeah, except now he looks in the waking world as I shaped him in the dream when I took his awareness from him so he would stop hurting. I changed him in real life from inside the dream. I don't know how, but that's why he couldn't shift. He tried to shift to his old form, but it died when he changed. He used the anger and frustration I had felt for him to force the shift to his new form. It spilled over the brink when Smoke became alarmed for my safety and reached for me. Smoke didn't know Griz was my bear," Melody said.

"I can see why Griz would feel guilty for attacking Smoke, but Smoke is centuries old. He's an unbonded alpha shifter. He knew better than to even consider touching you in front of another unbonded alpha shifter who thought you were his mate. Hell, I'm bonded, but if Smoke had reached for Eli, I would have ripped out his throat with my teeth. Eli's mine. I won't share her. All unbonded men feel like a threat to my direwolf. Imagining it has my wolf snarling too close to the surface," Luke said.

"Griz is precise in his honor. He feels he misread the situation from its inception. Although he originally felt justified in his behavior toward Smoke, Griz now believes his frustration with his magic caused it all. Griz felt as if we could've avoided it if he'd understood the situation more clearly. His honor demanded he apologize."

CHAPTER TWENTY-THREE

Think The Same

M^{*elody*}

*M*elody

"Griz was wounded. Smoke reached for you. Griz attacked Smoke to defend you. There was only one outcome. Griz has a highly defined code of honor if he still sees himself at fault in the situation. I imagine he prefers peace and balance as opposed to the destruction his magic makes him capable of. It seems to be a bear thing. Kallik is like-minded," Luke said.

"He believes rules for how people are to be treated exist to be followed," Melody said.

"Can you explain?" Eli asked.

"He wouldn't hear my refusal not to spend his money when we went out in the Hummer yesterday. I explained to him I didn't have the money to eat out. He stiffened for a bit. I thought he would rumble at me, but he looked at me sternly and informed me he wasn't a college-aged foolish boy. He didn't ask me to pay, nor would he ever. I got the impression I had somehow insulted his manhood, but I don't see how. Anyway, he informed me he would provide for me and warned me not to accept gifts from other men."

Melody explained what had made her think Griz saw his place in the dream by a prescribed set of rules. Fox nodded as if he agreed with Griz. Oddly, he wasn't the one Melody had thought was so old-fashioned.

"That sounds right. Eli can have anything she desires when we go out together, as long as she's using my money. What kind of man doesn't pay for the woman?"

He asked as if he couldn't imagine how low that man must be because Luke could never conceive of a situation in which he wouldn't provide for a woman.

"That's silly and so old-fashioned. Why does Eli work, if all she has to do is ask you for money?"

Melody asked him.

"She works because she enjoys her career. She gets fulfillment from it. It makes her happy. She is everything. Her happiness is my true life goal. She has her own money in case I'm unable to be with her. I wouldn't want her to miss an opportunity for something important because she was temporarily lacking access to my resources."

Luke seemed a little confused by the question.

"Are you saying Eli has complete freedom with your money? She can do whatever she wants with it?" Melody asked.

The man was insane.

"Of course. I worked for it because of her. I'm hers. Everything I have is hers. She is *everything*. If she needed me to give it all away, I would give it all away. My only question would be to whom should I give it?" Luke said.

His brow drew down.

"Give it up, Melody. We both know it makes no sense. It's an alpha male thing. Javier has been trying to give all his money to Isabell for over a week now. She keeps telling him to keep it, but he's dead set on finding a way to either give it all to her or spend it on her. The retreat at Draoithe is in my name as a silent partner, just so no one can take my home from me. I don't even live there," Eli said.

"Luke made Fox deed the Labyrinth to me after they agreed to build my art gallery, so no one could infringe upon my rights as a gallery operator because I would own it."

Isabell shook her head.

"When Duncan learned we might need vehicles, he ordered me two Teslas in case I crash one."

Artie rolled her eyes.

"You have two Teslas?" Melody asked.

She would never have enough money to buy half a Tesla, much less two of them.

"Yeah, it's silly. One was enough," Artie said.

"Are you not happy with one of them, Artie?" Fox asked.

He acted seriously eager to know.

"I can only drive one at a time. I would be happier with only one. Can I give the other one away?" Artie asked.

"Let me get the titles so you can decide which one you don't want. We'll sign it away immediately."

With that, he left the room for a minute and returned with both titles.

"Which will you keep, Artie?" Fox asked.

Artie plucked a title out of his hand.

"I'll keep this one."

"Did you have someone in mind to take possession of this one?" Fox asked.

"Melody doesn't have a vehicle. She could use it. May I give it to her?" Artie asked.

Fox signed the title and went to the key hanger, pulling off a set of keys. He handed both the title and the keys to Melody.

Artie smiled at Fox. She was happy. Fox was happy.

Melody was confused. Isabell, Eli, and Luke laughed. Fox picked Artie up out of her chair and kissed her soundly.

"Artie is *everything* to Fox. He'll deny her nothing. When she challenges him, he's never failed to prove that to her. They've been together for over four hundred years. If she told him the sky needed to be painted purple, I believe he'd make it happen so she would smile at him," Eli said.

Melody looked at the keys and the title of a Tesla. Fox had signed the title over to her. She owned a Tesla. It was the strangest scene she'd ever lived through.

"That's Artie's way of letting Fox know she values your friendship. If you're important to her, he'll move mountains to help you for her sake. When Elliot's men kidnapped me, I called Artie. Fox tracked me and came after me. He felt her fear for me," Isabell explained.

"Isabell, you know Fox collects strays. He loves you like his niece. I think rescuing you was a little of both combined with a serious real man complex. He couldn't have left you there. Regardless of either his feelings for you or Artie. He could affect your rescue, so he did it. Fox couldn't see himself as a man if he hadn't," Eli said.

"Fox is a king. He was born a king. He can't 'not' act like one. Fox was born touching Druid magic. It rules his life. Once you understand he can't lay it down or be any other way, you accept his idiosyncrasies. Fox is a good man."

Luke grinned at his friend's antics.

Fox's public attention embarrassed Artie. Melody smiled at the old fox couple. Then she looked at the keys to the Tesla again. She couldn't accept the gift. Griz could never deal with it.

"Fox co-owns Draoithe with Javier and me. Relax, he signs the titles for everyone's vehicles. Draoithe gave you the Tesla. Griz won't be angry. It's okay for you to keep it."

Luke must have read her nervousness.

"Consider it yours while you're here. If you leave, leave the title and the keys. If you stay, then it'll be part of your benefits package."

"Thank you. I don't know what to say," Melody said.

Luke wanted her to stay. Fox was in on it. Artie wanted to give her the car. Artie didn't want Melody to leave, either.

Artie was a kindred spirit. Melody liked Artie. Driving a car worth a literal living fortune appealed to the poor California girl Melody was.

"Say you'll drive with me to the grocery store tomorrow. I need to get out of here. I feel claustrophobic."

Artie smiled, and Melody nodded.

Melody wanted to stay at Draoithe. Everyone wanted her to stay. Luke had offered her the best job imaginable. The other women helped her fit in and built her into their lives.

It felt good to think it could be normal. She hoped Griz came to think the same.

CHAPTER TWENTY-FOUR

Serve The Ruiri

G *riz*

After breakfast, Griz kissed Melody and left her in the company of Artie and Isabell in the sunroom. Isabell was painting.

Griz needed to find Smoke. He wanted to make amends for having killed the dragon. He hadn't been himself.

Melody didn't understand. She'd felt threatened and shifted. Her owl accepted the destruction of the threat with relief. She thought Griz protected her.

His anger and frustration clouded his judgment. He should have found a better solution.

Griz preferred peace. He'd never known his father. It had been his mother who instilled in him at a young age that neither his size nor his magic should ever be a license for the use of destructive force. It was her gentle influence which made him the man he was.

Griz had failed to follow the wisdom he'd learned in his youth. He'd allowed his emotional state to determine his actions. This time, a man had died. It wasn't the first time Griz had killed a man, but it was the first time he felt guilty for it.

The man had been an invincible dragon, and Fox had the magic to restore Smoke. To see if he could stay, Griz needed to rectify his failure to maintain his control.

Griz had never been part of the group, but joining one where he'd already made enemies seemed like a bad idea. He deliberately left Melody with the ladies, so there would be no further issues with his bear's possessiveness about his mate.

He walked over to the next house and rang the doorbell. He heard a lot of shuffling and finally, the front door opened. The entire foyer had frozen over.

Griz frowned. It was July. The ceiling ice dripped onto the floor as the foyer melted.

The man at the door could've been Smoke's twin brother, except his hair was black, his eyes were green, and his face was different. Otherwise, Griz felt as if looked at the same man. Necromancy.

The man asked Griz if he could help him. Griz asked if Smoke might be available. Char invited Griz inside.

"Be careful. The doorbell startled Tessara. She accidentally froze all the water in the foyer in response. She's still a little jumpy. We're working on it, right Tessara?"

Char smiled at a little strawberry blonde-haired lady with lavender eyes. She smiled timidly back at Char and nodded.

"I'm Char. Who may I tell Smoke is here to see him?" Char asked.

"I'm Griz, the bear he met yesterday," Griz said.

Char laughed.

"I'll tell my brother you're here, but I doubt he'll be happy to meet with you after your last encounter."

"I came to apologize for my behavior," Griz said.

Char raised his eyebrow.

"It was his mistake, not yours. He owned it already. He's angry with himself, not you."

"It's a bit of a complicated story, but the whole encounter shouldn't have taken place as it did."

"He's in the dining room with Keira, Lightning, and Cloud. He says to invite you in. Have you had breakfast?" Char asked.

He waited for Tessara to precede him down the hall. Tessara smiled at Char and walked down the hallway. Char pointed to the foyer when two servants reported to him. They bowed and cleared the ice from the home's entryway.

"Yes, thank you," Griz replied.

He wasn't hungry. Nadine had toasted bagels with flavored cream cheeses, jams, sliced fruit, and nuts to top them, along with scrambled eggs, bacon, and sausages.

"Do you drink coffee or tea?" Char asked.

"Tea please," Griz said.

They made their way to the dining room.

Char introduced him to the others in the room. Smoke and another dragon brother, Lightning, sat next to Keira and Cloud as they finished breakfast. Smoke and Lightning rose to their feet when Griz entered the room.

"My king, how may we serve you?" Lightning asked.

He bowed to Griz.

It was a strange way to be greeted by the sandy-haired, ocean-blue-eyed man, but the dragons were strange, anyway. All of them looked like clones of the same man, which someone had replaced the face, hair, and eyes on.

The Necromancy was obvious. The shaman who'd made them was highly skilled.

"I came to apologize to Smoke," Griz said.

He looked the other man in the eyes.

"My lord, I don't understand."

Smoke looked bewildered.

He looked at his brothers. Char shrugged his shoulders as he served a cup of hot breakfast tea for Griz and held up a jar of honey.

Griz nodded. He was a bear. No bear turned down honey, even if it did sometimes get to Winnie-the-Pooh antics over the sweet stuff.

"I think an explanation is in order. Will you hear me out?" Griz asked.

Smoke nodded at a chair, and Griz took his tea from Char and sat down at the table. Lightning and Smoke resumed their chairs, and Char served himself and Tessara as they joined him at the table.

"Smoke, I'm sorry for what happened yesterday. I wasn't myself."

Griz paused and ran his hand over the back of his neck, organizing his thoughts.

"I was angry and frustrated with my inability to shift into my bear form. I'm still suffering from some lingering side effects from the drugs Elliot's men used to 'cure' me. My emotions clouded my judgment. I should never have been short with you. I falsely assumed things about you and completely misunderstood your words and behavior, which predicated the entire event. And I want to apologize for that," Griz explained.

"Griz, our king was right when he chastised me for reaching for your mate. The mistake was entirely mine," Smoke said.

"Our king?" Griz asked.

What was Smoke talking about? Did he mean Luke?

"Luke explained it to me afterward. It was my fault for not recognizing you. I recognized my queen Melody immediately. When you shifted, you didn't appear as I had last seen your bear. I became alarmed for the lady Melody's safety. It was my mistake, my king. Your apology isn't necessary."

Smoke dismissed the entire episode.

"Luke is your king?"

"He's the Ri ruirech of Draoithe. We've sworn fealty to him. We are, all of us, Dragon Knights and Protectors of the Realm," Smoke explained.

"Then it seems I must insist you accept my apology. If it was your job to protect Melody and you didn't recognize me, then I have twice crossed the line of acceptable behavior. Please accept my humble apology."

Griz felt even smaller than he had when he realized he was the one responsible for the debacle. Smoke had only done his job and protected the one woman Griz saw as *everything* to him.

"My king, brother, perhaps you should both accept that each of you had part responsibility for the misunderstanding and move forward. No one is worse off for it. Leave it in the past where it belongs."

Lightning addressed Griz and Smoke.

Smoke grinned at Griz and nodded. Griz smiled back at the dragon.

"Lightning, did you just call me 'your king'?"

Lightning nodded. Griz raised a brow at him.

"You're the last king. When you rise, I'll become your knight. I'm the protector of your stake in the realm," Lightning said.

"What are you talking about? I don't have a stake in the realm. I'm not part of all this."

Griz tried to make sense of things. Maybe the man had gotten Griz confused with someone else.

"Not yet, but you're mated to my future queen. Luke, Fox, and Javier already see you as Ruiri. You appeared in the mirror when Luke needed to see the truth about the dragons," Lightning said.

"Luke said something about Ruiri to me yesterday, but I have a choice in the matter."

Griz didn't like the idea his future wasn't his to decide. He'd been seriously thinking of applying for pack membership if the land was as nice as he believed. Had he they deceived him?

"My king, you must choose it, or Luke will seek another. We all believe it was you we saw in the glass. It's possible we made a mistake. You aren't as we originally saw you," Char stated simply.

"Griz, you're changed. There are two clear paths in front of you. Choose for your mate. She gave you back to yourself. She'll always be what saves you," Keira whispered.

Griz looked at the delicate-boned woman sitting next to Smoke. Her striking blue eyes framed by dark brown hair made her appear exotic. What did she mean?

"I don't think I follow your words, ma'am," Griz said.

"Melody is your everything. She'll need to leave your side. She'll walk through the wall for you. Choose your path for her sake. Choosing against Melody will cause you to be lost forever."

Keira tried to explain.

"I agree with you. Melody is *everything*, but I'm not sure I understand the rest," Griz said.

"I'm a Nephilim, and I watch the auras of others. I can only tell you what I see. When she walks through the wall for you, then you will know you must decide."

Keira smiled at Griz.

Griz nodded. He still wondered how Melody would walk through a wall.

"My king, how is it you're so changed? I didn't recognize your current form," Smoke said.

"I look exactly as I did before in this form. It's the bear which Melody altered. You saw me as a bear first. I'm confused about how you recognized me as a man," Griz asked.

"We're dragons. We have second sight, so we see what all immortals are. They can't hide from us because we can see them in all their forms," Char said.

"So, Smoke saw me as a different bear and thought I was someone else?" Griz asked.

"Exactly, my king, so how did you change?" Smoke asked.

"Melody did it. I was dying, and she met me in the dream. She's a bird shifter, and I'm her mate. I got lost in her when she tried to mesmerize me to lessen the pain. My physical body went into hibernation, and she stole my awareness. When she gave me back to myself, I was in the form I have now. She changed me in the dream and gave me some part of her bird magic. I trace in flames now. I think perhaps I faded, but she refused to let me go. Melody saved me, but it's why I wasn't my usual self when we first met," Griz said.

"I don't wish to make enemies. I would prefer peace."

"My king, that's why we believe you're the last king. You have no enemies among us. We're dragons; we serve the Ruiri," Smoke said.

CHAPTER TWENTY-FIVE
Pine Needles

G*riz*

"Thank you, my friend. It's good to know. Tell me, have you seen Draoithe?"

"It's the strangest of castles our new king has built, but it fits the grand style of a Ri ruirech of this time. The retreat is two stories. My queen, Eli, says it resembles an alpine ski lodge? The land is forested, clean, and wild. It's beautiful. The forest is untouched virgin land with two small lakes. Will you see it?" Lightning asked.

"Luke invited Melody and me to see the land this afternoon. I'm curious. I've been a rancher for most of my years in Colorado. Luke asked me about farming organic and running cattle. He's been kind enough to grant me sanctuary here. The least I can do is give him the advice he requested," Griz explained.

He itched to be in the wild outdoors. To feel the life of the surrounding forest was like a balm to his soul. Outside, no matter how extreme the weather might be, it was always preferable to indoors.

Griz wanted to feel the sun, the wind, and the rain. The heat or cold, and snow were where he wanted to live. He needed the wild like he needed Melody.

"I believe you'll like it, my king. It feels good to be there. Phase one should finish in a couple more weeks. Luke wishes to move in and settle the pack, and build phase two shortly," Lightning said.

"Thank you, gentlemen. Ladies, it's been a pleasure. I appreciate the hospitality. If you'll excuse me, I think I should take my leave."

Griz stood up to go.

"Thank you for coming. Your visit has been informative to us. If we can be of service in the future, please request our help."

Smoke clasped right forearms with Griz.

"Good day, gentlemen."

Griz nodded to the others, and Smoke showed him to the door.

When Griz stepped off the porch into the warm late morning sunshine, he felt better, but something bothered him. What the dragons said tickled his thoughts. Dragons could see immortals for what they were, no matter what form they took.

He walked down to the creek and across the bridge. He found an old pine with a nice bed of dry needles beneath the branches. Griz sat in the pine's shade and leaned his back against the pine's trunk. He wanted to remember.

He'd met a man like the dragons before. Griz searched his memories. There had been a man at the bar the Thursday night he'd stopped for a drink.

The man had seemed odd, but Griz had had a few drinks. He had celebrated finding his mate in the dream. He hadn't been drunk, but he'd felt pretty good.

The man had accidentally bumped into Griz as Griz left. He remembered thinking the man felt wrong, but had just thought the man overindulged and stumbled. He'd ignored the incident.

Griz recalled nothing from that point until he woke up in a cage in the damn warehouse. Griz rumbled. There were still holes in his recollection which needed filling.

He tried to recall the drunk again. The man looked up at Griz, smiled a toothy grin, and slurred an apology. Griz nodded and walked into the night.

The man had pointed teeth as Smoke had as a dragon. Griz wondered. Could the man have been a dragon, too?

He sat thinking about it. If what Char had said was true of any dragon, then it would explain how someone would've known what he was.

It would explain how all those women had become captives. A dragon, who would recognize them for what they were, may have stalked them.

Did Elliot have a dragon walking around identifying immortals? It would explain a lot.

Griz pulled out the cell phone Luke gave him and opened it. He sent a text message to Luke.

Are there other dragons besides the ones who serve you? - Griz.

I'm not sure. Let me ask Fox. He may have a better answer. Why? - Luke.

I don't know yet. I'm still thinking about it. - Griz.

Fox says there were others, but until we met Ash, he'd assumed they were all gone. No one had identified any for about three hundred years. Let me know what you figure out? - Luke.

Sure thing. Thanks. - Griz.

If the dragons he'd met sought Luke and the Druid pack, what if others had done something similar? It hadn't been hard for seven dragons to show up at Draoithe.

He didn't have enough information about dragons. He shelved his line of reasoning. It was a good jump-off point for a conversation with Fox and a dragon later.

He needed to understand how he had gotten to the current point in his life. He meditated.

The heat of the summer surrounded him as he sat in the shade. He'd found Melody in the dream. He'd visited her in the dream for days.

More than a week had passed when she would finally speak to him. He'd been on cloud nine.

The Thursday when Griz went into captivity, he'd finished his chores in the barn when his boss asked him to drive into Boulder and pick up some things at the hardware store. It had been out of the ordinary, but not unheard of.

The list included saw blades, sandpaper, wood screws, wood glue, polyurethane wood sealer, and several sizes and types of lumber. Griz hadn't questioned the list. He'd simply accepted it, got into the ranch's work truck, and left for Boulder at two-thirty in the afternoon.

It was a little over an hour into Boulder, and he'd made it to Home Depot around three forty-five. He loaded the truck with lumber and supplies enough to build a rather large deck by four-thirty.

Griz stopped to eat. He rarely indulged himself in eating out, but he was in Boulder. He might not be back again for weeks.

After a good meal, Griz had stopped at the one bar he preferred on the way out of Boulder. He'd bought a few shots in between a few beers and talked to the bartender. They'd known one another for at least fifteen years.

Griz hadn't been drunk. He probably should've drunk less, but he'd eaten well. Griz had slowly finished his last beer while he waited for his shifter metabolism to counteract the effects of the alcohol.

He studied the scene in his mind. The drunk who'd stumbled into him had been sitting at a table in the corner with a couple of other men.

There were three of them. Griz remembered thinking they had been triplets out for a drink. They looked similar. The way all the dragons looked similar.

Griz felt certain the men who kidnapped him were dragons, too. He couldn't prove it, of course, but it would've made sense. If the drunk had stumbled into him and nicked him with a drug, Griz may not have noticed. The shock of being bumped into unexpectedly likely covered it.

Griz had no memory of ever reaching the truck. His boss had told Griz the police had found it and called him two mornings later when the bar manager contacted them about towing it.

If he'd collapsed, it would've taken several powerful men to lift him and make off with him. The dragons could've done it, but it would've been difficult for four humans to do it. If the triplets at the bar were dragons, then Griz knew he had his suspects.

The question was, why him? Why take Griz? All the other captives had been women as far as he could tell.

Did his captors want a bear shifter or a dreamwalker specifically? Had they targeted him, or had he merely been in the wrong place at the right time?

He tried to focus past all the pain and anger which consumed him after he noticed himself in the cage.

What had his captors done or said? Were there any clues there?

They'd dragged him out of the cage when they realized he regained consciousness from the drugs they'd given him. Whatever they'd given him had left him groggy, disoriented, and uncoordinated. Griz fought back, but he could barely defend against the blows.

They stripped his strength away. They'd beaten him and kicked him repeatedly until he shifted into his bear form.

He remembered them saying something about testing a cure on him. Griz wasn't sick. He'd been born a shifter. In his long life, he'd never been sick. It was a by-product of immortality.

They injected him with something which made him ill. His bear magic had reacted violently. He'd traced back and forth in the light between forms uncontrollably for a long while. He'd passed out at some point.

He came to himself again at a later point, much weaker than he'd been before. He'd smelled the women then. That was when he saw the man they called Rake.

He'd watched Rake assault the women. Griz had listened as his captors laughed and joked about them. He'd tasted the women's fear in the air.

It enraged him. He roared his fury and tried to break away from his captors.

They beat him relentlessly while chained to a table of some sort. They injected him again with the same drug as before.

The uncontrollable shifting started again. He grew weaker. Griz bled, and his magic couldn't heal his battered body. He'd wanted to fade.

He couldn't break free. Griz couldn't help the women. He ached and hurt. Griz couldn't help himself.

Then they injected him with something which burned. He seized, and his memory blanked.

He knew they continued dosing him with drugs, forcing him to seize repeatedly. But of his accurate memory, there was nothing.

When he woke, he knew his death was near. If he faded, he would no longer feel guilty his strength had failed him and failed others. Then he saw Melody.

Was he awake? She'd come to him in the dream. She'd taken him away from it all and shut his body down. He'd woken up lying beside her when she gave him back to himself.

He didn't understand why they'd wanted to cure him. They wanted to stop him from shifting. They had focused on his bear.

His being a dreamwalker had mattered little. It was his immortal magic they intended to strip away from him or block from his use. He still wondered why?

Griz left his thoughts once they circled. It was past one in the afternoon. He needed some lunch and to see Melody again. He rose and headed back to Fox's house after shedding the pine needles from his jeans.

CHAPTER TWENTY-SIX

His Disapproval

M^{elody}

Melody caught her breath when Griz stepped into the dining room. He was strikingly handsome. He wore a heavy cotton button-down men's shirt with the sleeves rolled up. Griz tucked it into his jeans, and his belt looked good above his hips, around a narrow waist.

Hello Handsome. Melody thought.

I'm glad you like the way I look, snowbird. I'm starving, but I think the dragons may have helped me figure out some missing pieces. Did you eat already?

Oh, I hadn't meant for you to hear my thoughts. Yes, I um...

He smiled as she blushed her embarrassment. He teased her. She could feel his amusement. He seemed more relaxed, but hungry.

She stood up from the table and rinsed her plate. Melody joined Griz as he stepped behind the breakfast bar to make some sandwiches. She helped him stack several slices of bread with meats, cheeses, and sliced vegetables.

He smiled at her, but he talked to Luke and Fox. Melody didn't mind. He was her bear.

Luke

"Griz, did you figure anything out?" Luke asked.

Fox looked up, curious.

"I think the men who took me were dragons or something like them. When I spoke to Smoke, Char, and Lightning earlier, Smoke explained how he should've recognized me. Because Melody had altered me, he'd suspected my being with her. After I left, I got to thinking about the events which led to me being trapped in a cage. A necromancer made the dragons. So they feel wrong to me as a dreamwalker."

Griz ate and explain at the same time. Melody served Griz more tea. Luke saw Griz smile at her. It was good to see Griz acknowledge Melody's care for him.

"Kallik had similar misgivings about them," Luke recalled.

"I've felt the same wrongness in others before. In Boulder the night they kidnapped me, I'd stopped at a bar for some drinks after dinner. It was a little over an hour's drive back to the ranch after I'd gotten supplies. Pleased with myself after having found Melody in the dream, I celebrated because it would likely be weeks before I was back in town. I talked to the bartender for a while. I don't think he was in on it. We've known each other for fifteen years."

Griz thought about it. Luke could see he questioned the bartender's role in what had happened, but Griz believed the bartender was an innocent.

"I remembered seeing three men sitting at a table drinking. The sight of three drunken men sitting at a table had amused me. They had all looked the same. The way the dragons do. I sipped my last beer, waiting for my metabolism to counter the effects of the alcohol before I left to drive back. I wasn't drunk when I left the bar."

Griz was emphatic at that point. Fox and Luke nodded their acceptance of his statement as a fact. Shifters could drink a lot, and the effects wore off quickly. Drinking didn't equal being drunk.

"One triplet stumbled and bumped into me as I left. I stepped back, startled. He grinned at me as he slurred his apology. I ignored the drunken man, but I remember thinking his smile was odd, as if he had pointed teeth. I'd been drinking, so I dismissed the clues about a dangerous situation, and I never made it to the truck."

Griz rumbled low at his foolishness. He shook his head and continued.

"Now, if dragons can see me as I am, and there are seven of them here, why couldn't three of them be at a bar in Boulder? They focused on me being a shifter because they tried to 'cure' me. What I can't figure out is why? And whether they knew I would be there, or if they just got lucky when I stopped for a drink?" Griz said.

"Fox, do you think Elliot uses dragons to target people? Is this a realistic possibility?" Luke asked.

He wanted information. Knowledge was power.

"Griz is right. There were once lots of dragons in Europe. The petty kings had shamans making them before Christianity spread. They were a way to merge power. It would've been the reason my ancestor's predecessor king had our seven dragons made to start with. The last lead I had on the whereabouts of any dragons following the fall of my kingdom fizzled out and went cold after I met Artie. Most of the kingdoms crumbled to the new nationalism sweeping Europe because of the Hundred Years' War," Fox explained.

"The seven you knew still exist. So it's entirely possible others still exist, too. Maybe some found an ally in Elliot." Luke said.

Isabell paled as the conversation continued.

Melody grew concerned for Isabell and asked her if she was alright. Isabell looked at her and turned to Griz.

"Griz, what did the men look like, the ones you called triplets?" Isabell asked.

"All three were about five foot eleven, about Javier's height. I remember looking down at them slightly. They all had the same weight and build, too. They were stockier than Javier, brown hair and green eyes, slightly hawkish noses."

"I saw them in my art gallery in California. They came to look at some pieces the night I fell asleep in my studio. What are the chances three nearly identical triplets fitting Griz's description would show up at my gallery on the night of my kidnapping and be a coincidence?" Isabell asked, then shuddered.

"We seem to have a new piece of the puzzle thanks to Griz and Isabell. Your remembering is enough proof for me to add dragons to our working theory on Elliot. Let me call Ash. I want to know if our dragons can add to this," Luke said.

Lily came through the back door.

"Luke, Ryker sent me to ask, how many vehicles do you need ready for the trip to Draoithe this afternoon? Also, I wondered if I could tag along. I wanted to see the restaurant again. I had this great idea for an alfresco outdoor dining experience. Ryker said Isabell would go, and I hoped she might sketch something for me?" Lily asked.

Isabell smiled and nodded as Luke answered Lily.

"Ask him to have three lined up. I think nine of us are going now." Luke smiled at Lily.

Lily spoke to Ash and Raven as they passed one another on the deck. Lily ran off to talk with Ryker as Ash and Raven stepped through the door.

Raven nodded timidly to all the people in the room and shrank into Ash. Luke could tell the alphas in the room intimidated her. Ash hugged her and moved so Raven could sit next to Melody and Artie at the table.

"My king, how may I assist you?"

Ash grasped forearms with Luke. Luke scowled at Ash's formal language.

"Ash, just call me Luke," Luke groused.

Ash lowered his white head.

"Sorry, old habits."

"Ash, what do you know about a group of triplet dragons?" Fox asked.

"The only triplets I knew were not agreeable to me," Ash said, scowling, remembering.

"Why?"

"Griz and Isabell both had previous experiences with triplets before their abductions. Griz thinks they felt to him as you do, wrong," Luke said.

"You're the product of necromancy. It has a uniquely odd feel to a dreamwalker. You're not in the dream as others are. You're like a ghost in the dream," Griz explained.

"And these triplets you met before were the same?" Ash questioned.

"Yes, but I'd never met a dragon before, and I'd been drinking. I dismissed the feeling, putting it down to the effects of the alcohol."

Griz admitted his mistake.

"I questioned how Elliot identified the immortals he kidnapped. If he had dragons working for him, it would explain a lot. If it is the three I'm thinking of, we may face a threat," Ash said.

"Out with it," Luke demanded.

"Inferno is their Lord. Blast and Pyro are his clones. They're nearly black themselves. The necromancer who made them chose not to...aaah..." Ash trailed off, uncomfortable.

"Chose not to do what?" Griz demanded.

"Ladies, will you excuse us? Griz, Ash, will you join us in the library?" Luke requested.

Griz finished the last sandwich on his plate. When he stood up, Melody reached to take his plate, but Griz rumbled softly at her. She sat back down.

He kissed her hair and rinsed his plate. He served himself another glass of tea and carried it down the hall, following Ash and Fox to the library. Luke marked the scene.

Griz liked Melody taking care of him, but he refused to allow her to be his servant. Griz had manners.

Melody smiled when he rumbled at her. It was a gentle acknowledgment of her desire to cater to him, but his disapproval of it.

CHAPTER TWENTY-SEVEN
The Day Wore On

L^{uke}

Griz and Melody were still learning about each other. Melody was young. Griz may have slightly old-fashioned ideas about how men should treat women, but he held Melody in high regard. He would fit in at Draoithe. Luke wanted him as the last Ruiri.

When the four men sat in the library, Luke looked at Ash.

"Explain it," Luke ordered.

"He chose not to break them as men," the dragon lord whispered.

"They have no safeguard against harming those weaker than themselves."

"They lack honor?" Fox questioned.

"They're loyal. They aren't oath breakers, but they can kill a woman or a child without regard. I can not."

"Luke, it's difficult to speak of. Forgive my reticence. My brothers and I came with safeguards. We were all knights, warriors, who had fought and died in battle. The shaman dragged our souls from the Underworld and forced them to live again as dragons. I don't know the caliber of character

147

we had as men. None of us can recall. We don't remember our lives before. Char feels familiar to me, but I have lost the memory of how I might have known him. Did we offer mercy to the fallen? Slake our desires on unwilling women? Did we beat the helpless?"

Ash shrugged.

"So, when you became dragons, a shaman made you to be the men you are?" Fox asked.

"The shaman broke us all. We know what it is to be forced by a man. We empathize with the plight of the weak and the helpless. My brothers and I have great magic, but I cannot strike a child or hurt a woman. I cannot fight a bound man, nor one who is unarmed or unskilled. Magic prevents it. I don't know whether I always thought that way, or if I succumbed to the will of the magic. I believe it's the way a real man behaves. Anything else is reprehensible. My brothers are the same," Ash explained.

Luke, Fox, and Griz all nodded. It was good to know they believed the same way.

"These three dragons you spoke of. How were they made differently?" Luke asked.

"Yes, they're servants, as I am, but they remained unbroken. I had to wait for my riders to come to me. They kept thralls. Women fed dragon blood like a drug. The women will do anything to get the blood again. Dragons have to store energy from sex to fly. Inferno once used a woman repeatedly until she died to store enough energy to fly across Europe into Russia with no need to stop."

Ash grimaced. Luke and Fox growled, and Griz rumbled.

"Elliot has three immoral dragons working with him. We need to prevent them from hunting immortals. Ash, how can we stop them?" Luke asked.

"Dragons can't die true death. We're invincible. Dragons fear only the Valkyries. A Valkyrie could use my spear to stab me through the heart and release the magic of the Netherworld. I would disintegrate into ashes. Even then, she would have to do it on orders from the Ri ruirech or the Ruiri. If you didn't order her to kill me, she wouldn't do so," Ash said.

"But, I killed Smoke," Griz said.

"Death is only temporary for dragons. If I hadn't brought Smoke back, his soul would have fled to the Netherworld until his body regenerated at dawn. They lack the coins to pay the ferryman at the River Styx. With the rising sun, he would've returned to himself, but he would've suffered from memory loss. For every hour of death he suffers here, he loses a day of his memories in the Netherworld. He would have lost a few weeks when he came back if I hadn't called him back. It wouldn't have been good for Keira, or I might've left him for not thinking."

The situation with Smoke still aggravated Fox. Ash nodded.

"Fox, how did you call Smoke back?" Luke asked.

"Druid magic is from the Netherworld. It originally animated Smoke when his soul came back and joined his dragon in corporal form. So all I had to do was to draw on that magic and whisper his name when I sent it into his body. It isn't what allows him to shift and fly. That's pure sedr magic. Magic derived from the energy created during sex. Shifter magic is a blend of sedr magic and blood magic. It's complicated. You need to take classes and study it," Fox said.

Griz shook his head. Luke grinned at Fox. Ash nodded. Fox didn't want to give all the information he had because it only created more questions.

"One question, can Druid magic hold a dragon's soul in the Netherworld instead of allowing it to return to its body at dawn?" Luke asked.

"I don't know," Fox said.

Luke looked at Ash.

"I don't know, either. I'm sorry."

"Table it for now. I'll speak to Mihaela, Nadine, and Lily about adding more layers of protective shields to Draoithe since we know about this threat. If we can stop these dragons, we can curtail Elliot's plans. Griz, I have a few phone calls to make. Are we still on to see the land?" Luke asked.

"Sure thing. I'll check to see if Melody is ready," Griz said.

"Luke, may I accompany you? It would do Raven good to get out and move around more," Ash asked.

"Sure. It will be her home soon enough. Perhaps she can decide on furnishings for her space. I believe the personal quarters are nearing completion. They're installing the light-blocking shades upstairs. The kitchen appliances will arrive next week. We can take a tour," Luke said.

Ash nodded. Fox left him in the library to make his calls. Luke contacted his designer and let her know he would send some more sketches for some more structures and asked if she could get back to him with some designs. Ursala's email reply assured him it was no problem, and she thanked him for continuing to do business with her.

Luke contacted Frank Grimes, the contractor, and asked to schedule a meeting next week to negotiate a new contract with his crew for the next phase of construction projects.

Frank penciled him in for next Tuesday at nine in the morning. Better early than late. It would be hot as the day wore on.

CHAPTER TWENTY-EIGHT
Motioned The Ladies

G*riz*

"I like the feel of the land. The house fits. It's a nice spread. Is it all like this?" Griz asked.

They walked up to the hill overlooking the lake.

"No, we added forty-five acres. There is an old stone well and a cleared field on the back of that area. Javier and I found it when we scouted it. Do you want to look?" Luke asked.

"How far away is it?"

They passed a stone circle which grew Griz's attention even as Javier answered him.

"This is where we handle submission ceremonies and swear the fealty oaths. The cleared land is probably a five to seven-minute walk through the trees, just past the edge of the second smaller lake."

"Yeah, let's see it. I see what you aim to do. If you built the retreat cabin suites out along a path around the smaller lake, you could create horse trails in this direction. If you left twenty-five acres separate as pasture, you could probably run about twelve head of cattle, but it isn't likely to be enough beef. You would need to double that. I still want to see the cleared land. If we tilled it for crops, that might be wiser. You could always lease pasture to graze cattle if you want it."

Griz thought out loud.

"Luke, what if we bought the pasture land next to this land? It's already fenced for cattle and has a pond. The barn's in rough shape, and the old house is shabby. We could tear down the existing structures and rebuild them to Griz's standards. That would solve the pasture problem."

Javier's suggestion had Luke taking out his phone to text both Smoke and Char to look into buying the pasture next to Draoithe. They continued walking past the smaller lake Javier wanted to stock with fish. The lengths to which both men intended to go to convince Griz to stay shocked him.

"A few piers and some picnic areas with a small stable for horses would make this a good stop on a horseback riding expedition. You could ride over, grab a pole, fish, and enjoy the catch of the day over your fire. Then ride back to the main stables before dark. It would make a good outdoor recreation spot."

Fishing excited Javier.

They reached the clearing with the old stone wall and a well, and Griz fell in love. Someone had tilled about five flat acres some years past. The soil looked good. He'd seen a sizable greenhouse back at Draoithe's main house.

He could start the plants there, bring out some draft horses and a plow, till, and grow an oversized vegetable patch. It would need to be fenced to keep out squirrels and rabbits, but he could see the potential. If the well had water, he could use it for irrigation in the hot, dry summer months.

Luke's phone beeped with a message.

"Char says it's up for sale. The pasture property has been for sale for a while, but the man wants too much for it."

"Let's drive-by on the way back. Me, you, Griz, Isabell, and Melody can stop and see if Griz thinks it will work. How many acres is it?" Javier asked.

"Char says it's just shy of fifty-five acres. That would get us about twenty-five head of cattle. We could run maybe five dairy cows and twenty for beef. We could keep goats on the wooded twenty acres here. I'm thinking we cut out ten or fifteen acres of forest and replace it with an orchard and let the goats keep the rows clear," Luke said.

"That's not a bad idea. It would take a few years before you got a fantastic fruit harvest, but you could grow berries, grapes, and nuts. We could keep hives out near the orchard to produce honey and guarantee pollination. It would be all organic. We'd need more horses. The barns will supply the fertilizer, and we can install a solar pump at the stone well during the dry season for irrigation. We already have small livestock, but ducks or geese would be good, too. How many hens do we have?"

If they had enough rabbits and hens, they could supply extra meat for the restaurant that way as well. Griz could build up rabbit stock relatively easily.

"I think we have twenty right now, and we have fifteen rabbits."

"Has Eli got a rooster?"

Animal husbandry would be a challenge at first, but once things worked, it would become a routine. Luke shook his head about the roosters.

If they wanted to avoid purchasing more hens, they would need a rooster or two. As large as the pack was, two hen houses would probably be better. He figured he could fence a couple of three-acre sections of forest and build the hen houses inside, letting the hens wild-forage for most of the year. That would be more cost-effective, and the eggs would be of better quality.

"Well, we're gonna need two."

Griz studied the land.

If he could see the pasture and decide to place the barn, it would be well worth selling out of Colorado. There were many people, but there was also enough space to find peace. He could work outdoors as he wanted. He could run his operation as he'd always wanted.

"So if we could buy pasturage, you think we could make this a go? I mean, turn Draoithe into a near self-sufficient organic farmstead?" Luke asked.

"I think so. It would be a lot of work. It would probably be three to five years before it reached full potential, but it would be well worth the investment of time and money in the end."

Griz knew it would work as long as Luke didn't expect instant results. He could get out of the land what he needed for Draoithe, well, except maybe coffee. Griz would think about it and talk to Melody. He would need to sell the land he owned in Colorado as well.

"Let's head back and see if the others are ready to go. I need to speak with Fox, Lightning, Char, and Ember," Luke said.

Javier nodded. Griz took one last look around and turned and walked back with them.

"How many horses do we need for farm work?" Luke asked.

"One to ride, two to haul. Just for me. If we hire hands, they'll need horses, too."

He would need a horse to ride around the place every day, and he would need two to plow and haul materials, livestock, tools, seedlings, and produce. He needed a cart, a harness, and a plow.

Half the year was over, and the fencing was an incomplete job, nor was a barn even built. It would be a lot of work. Long hours outdoors. Griz would need help.

"Let's see the pasture. If the buildings are in disrepair, the fences are likely broken as well."

They passed by the stone circle, and Griz could feel the hallowed ground aura from it.

"You're probably right."

Javier had thought the same.

They stepped out of the trees to a scene from a nightmare.

Circling above Draoithe were three dragons. Griz heard Fox tell Lily to bring Nadine and Kallik along with some staves. He watched Lily wink out of Draoithe. A few minutes later, Lily, Nadine, and Kallik blinked into Draoithe. Seeing the teleportation disconcerted him.

Lily turned to Raven and grabbed her hand, and Nadine hugged Artie. The four women disappeared. Artie and Raven were too weak. No magic for them. Andrei and Ryker would stay with them and the others.

Griz walked up next to Melody, and Javier stopped beside Isabell. Luke stepped up next to Fox and Ash. Kallik handed the three staves to them. The triplets landed in the driveway.

Their riders dismounted and held clothing for the dragons, who shifted into men. Melody and Isabell looked away as the men dressed.

Griz looked at Isabell, who just nodded. These were the three she'd seen. They were the triplets Griz had seen as well. Griz and Javier both motioned the ladies to back away and shift so they could fly.

CHAPTER TWENTY-NINE

Seen It

G*riz*

"We've come for the bear. We tracked him here. Hand him over, and we'll be on our way," the lead man said.

"Griz, do you wish to go with these men?" Luke asked.

How had they tracked him? He would have to deal with that later. Griz realized Luke played a game. He didn't know what it was, but Griz played along with the alpha male.

"I do not!"

"I'm sorry, gentlemen. You wasted a trip. Griz stays. You may go now."

Luke dismissed the three as if he didn't have time to deal with them. They impeded Griz from seeing a potential pasture site, so his anger rose to the surface. He felt the anger Melody had given him. He might need it.

"The bear is necessary for our research," the man said.

"My friend isn't a lab rat. I warned you to leave. Heed the warning. I don't like trespassers."

Seriously irritated at having his home invaded, Luke spoke coldly, with no emotion.

His mind was still. It was strange to meet someone else who inverted the dream that way. Griz knew the place Luke stepped into. Luke intended violence against the three men. Griz had stepped into the same place to kill Smoke.

He stepped into the stillness as well. If Luke could kill them, he would. These three had harmed his friends, either directly or indirectly.

Griz would fight next to Luke. He wouldn't be a captive again.

"Who are you to give orders to a Lord of Dragons?" the man asked.

"Look, Inferno, I doubt you're a lord of anything. Just go back to your puppet master and admit defeat. You won't be taking anyone from here."

Luke didn't give up information, but he let the dragon know he knew who he was and who he worked for. Griz grinned. Let Elliot figure it out. It was a masterful game of chess.

The dragons and their riders had spears. They advanced towards the group. They faced off against one another in the driveway. Inferno recognized Ash. He stopped a few paces away.

"Ash, it has been a long time since we last met."

Inferno grinned a toothy dragon smile.

"Not long enough," Ash said.

"Four hundred years and you're still upset we borrowed your rider?"

Inferno laughed along with his brothers.

"Ash, tell this man what we are and have him hand over the bear. You can go back to crying over your long-lost lover as soon as we leave."

One brother chimed in.

"You didn't steal her. You killed her, Pyro."

Ancient anger vibrated in Ash's sneered response.

"This man knows what you are. He's denied your request; you may go."

"Stole her. Killed her. What does it matter? She was mortal. We helped her die faster. It was four centuries ago. Let it go already. You no longer have any authority. Give up the bear."

Blast tossed the words at Ash like a challenge.

"Take him if you think you can."

Luke ended the back and forth. The time for talking was over. The dragon fire rolled over all four dragons. Luke didn't hesitate to join the fight with Inferno. His staff clicked hard against the dragon's spear. Ash and Pyro were well-matched.

Griz jumped at Blast. The three riders attacked Kallik, Javier, and Fox. The spears clashed against staves and claws. Neither side seemed to have an edge. Griz inverted the dream and saw a solution. Did Luke see it?

I see the way. Do you trust me?

Luke's thoughts echoed in Griz's head.

I can stop these dragons. Do you want some revenge?

I see what you see because I inverted the dream as well. I want a reckoning!

Griz thought back as he sidestepped Blast's punch. He moved through the dream too fast for the dragon to comprehend what had happened.

Can you move fast enough to knock him down when Ash and I take down the other two?

Luke asked Griz.

Yeah, coordinate it with Ash. I can follow your lead.

Griz hoped Luke could do it. If he could make things work, the dragons would be toast. They wouldn't be kidnapping any more people for Elliot's ridiculous experimentation or unnecessary cures.

Griz kept Blast busy for a few more minutes. He taunted the slower dragon.

Then Ash and Luke switched tactics and ran at the other's opponent, slamming the staves down to the ground and using them to leap into the air over the heads of their opponents.

Griz stepped through the dream and landed on top of Blast about a half-second after Luke and Ash landed on Pyro and Inferno. The six of them went down to the ground, hard.

"Kallik, would you mind?!"

"Javier, freeze the women!"

Javier threw the frozen flames at the women. It coated them in ice. It began melting instantly, but it bought them the time they needed.

"Freeze, please."

Kallik rumbled as he swatted away one of the rider's attacks with his bear paw. The three dragons froze, just as the ice rained down on the women riders.

"Fox, can you do it?!"

Fox nodded. He no longer looked like the quiet librarian. Fox was the alpha king. He was the Fox whom Artie didn't wish to upset by talking to unbonded men.

Griz had only seen glimpses of the real Fox until then. Strangely, Griz liked the man better as the king he was. Javier jumped over the frozen spear, aimed at him, grabbed it, and pushed it back at the rider. He had to get out of the way.

The three women were melting fast, but it was too late. Fox stole their minds, and they trance-walked over to Ash and knelt on the ground in front of him. Ash looked perplexed.

"Tell Elliot he will have to find another way to hunt immortals. The immortals are now hunting for him. He would do well to run and hide."

Luke spoke to the wide-eyed frozen dragons while they lay on the floor as he, Ash, and Griz stood before them.

"Will you follow the orders of your king, Dragon Lord?"

He gave Elliot information, but not enough. Luke knew Elliot linked minds with the three dragons.

Luke waited for Ash, whose eyes were wide. The dragon nodded. He had sworn his fealty oath. He would obey his king.

"I wish you to turn these women. They are oath breakers. They're traitors," Luke said.

Ash immediately bit each woman on the shoulder in quick succession. They were women.

He had no choice but to follow the order. The magic forced him. He had sworn his oath.

The women fell to the ground in agony and rose as partial Valkyries. They had their fangs. The magic would never finish.

Ash stared, dumbfounded. He hadn't expected it. It was wrong. Griz knew it wasn't how a Valkyrie should exist.

The guilt over his role weighed on Ash. Griz felt it too, but he knew it was the way to achieve the reckoning he needed.

"Fox, if you'll be so kind as to send these back to their dragons. I have a pasture my friend wishes to see."

Griz grinned a fierce grizzly bear grin. The triplets got the end they deserved. Griz got his reckoning.

The three women each brandished their spears like pikes as they stood up and walked back to the three dragons. They drove the spears into the dragons' hearts. The dragons turned to ash, and the women collapsed as they burst into flames.

Fox slumped, and Luke caught him.

"Too much, old friend?"

Luke asked as Javier moved to take some of Fox's weight on his shoulders.

"Harder than I thought after they became Valkyries."

He breathed hard.

Using his Druid magic on three women at once must have taken a lot out of Fox. Griz wished it had not drained Fox so much. The mask Fox wore slipped back into place. He was once again the librarian.

Griz missed the king. He realized then that many at Draoithe had secrets and they all suffered. He wasn't alone, as one in need of the sanctuary Draoithe sought to provide. Even the men who owned it needed it.

Ash collected the dragon spears. They were dangerous to all but another dragon, the Valkyries, and the *den lasair*.

"How did you know that would work?" Kallik asked.

"I didn't. The magic forced me to act. The minute Griz stated he didn't wish to go with them, I had to protect him. He has a sanctuary. The magic made the demands that matched my intent. I could see it."

Luke shook his head, knowing his words didn't adequately explain.

"Ash, I'm sorry if I interpreted the rules for killing dragons differently than you explained them."

Griz looked at the dragon. It was obvious he struggled with the role he'd played. He felt guilty over turning the women.

Griz understood. It had been the only way. But harming women felt wrong. Griz had seen it, too.

CHAPTER THIRTY

Kissing His Owl

Griz

They helped Fox into the Hummer. Kallik got in to drive. Isabell and Melody slipped into another vehicle still in bird form, and Ash offered to take Isabell and Melody home.

Ash was quiet as he wrestled with his conscience. The women wouldn't shift back without clothes. Griz didn't want to part from Melody, but she needed to go.

Javier left his truck at Draoithe. He rode with Luke and Griz to see the pasture. Griz got down from the Hummer to look around with the two alpha males. The barn and the house and a small shed stood abandoned, and the barn rotted into ruins. Half the fence posts looked broken or warped.

The land itself was flat grassland. There were two ponds. That was even better. Griz grinned. He wanted it. He could add it to what they had. The fresh air stole the adrenaline from the fight. He relaxed.

Luke's phone beeped. He read his text message out.

"Char wants to know if we would like for him to negotiate for the land. He thinks we should get a discount as it is too close to the property, which seems to be infested with rogue dragon ashes."

"I swear, Ash sure can ruin a good story with that damn collar. Damn mind meddling dragons," Luke grumbled.

Javier laughed at his friend's aggravation.

"You're just miffed Fox's taking the starring role in the tale when it was all your idea. Don't worry. Eli will still prefer your huff and puff, and that's all that matters, my wolfish friend."

Griz grinned at the antics of the two dire wolves. They let the stress from the confrontation dissipate, but it was good to see them come out on top.

Some men took excess adrenaline out on others. That always wound up badly. Griz liked the two direwolves.

"What do you think, Griz? We buy the land, you run the ranch. The pay is $80,000 a year salary. You run the show, decide the hours, and order supplies. Draoithe pays for transportation, cell phone, clothes, room, and board. You join the pack, and the job is yours," Luke said.

Griz shook his head.

"No deal. If I join the pack, I want to be part owner of Draoithe. I'll be a silent partner. I don't want to know how you run the retreat or the other businesses, but I don't want to build up the ranch and put my sweat into the land to walk away in the future. Deal me in or no deal."

Griz had to play the game straight. If he did it, he wanted it done right. He needed to have a stake in it.

"I can't do it that way. The corporation has shares. Only one for each seat at the Guardian's table. If you join the pack, one is yours if you commit to becoming Ruiri and accepting Melody as your Ri bannach. We'll grant her one as well. This way, you would be equal partners with the pack leadership team."

"Let me discuss it with Melody. I'll give you my decision after I speak with her."

Griz didn't want to commit to anything until he knew Melody's heart on the matter.

"Let's go. I'm starving. You can talk to Melody while we eat," Javier said.

They drove back to Fox's house.

Griz got out of the Hummer and started toward the front door. He stopped in the driveway. He stared at the house.

Melody stepped through the wall to get to him. She phased through the wall like a ghost and solidified as she walked up to him. She had left him and then walked through a wall to him just like Angel said she would.

"Griz?" Melody asked.

"Melody, how did you do that?" Griz asked her.

"I don't know exactly, but it seems cool. I went through the door to the room without opening it first when I got here because I wanted to grab my sweater when I felt cold. The shock got to me. I stood in the room when I realized I had phased through the door. I heard the Hummer pull into the driveway, and I tried it with the wall."

"You walked through a wall to get to me?" Griz asked as he tried to take it all in.

That was important. He knew it was. Angel had told him to decide based on Melody. He couldn't protect her alone. Today was proof of that. He needed Luke, Kallik, Ash, and Fox that afternoon.

Melody smiled and nodded at his question. She was young, beautiful, sexy, and talented. She was his mate, and she was everything. He could be happy anywhere as long as he had her. He understood Angel's vision then.

"Melody, do you want to stay? I'll take you anywhere you want to go if you say you want to leave. I'll always protect you, and I'll provide for you, but I need to know what your heart wants. Do you want to stay?"

Griz searched her eyes. He looked into her soul, lost in her. The only thing he ever wanted was Melody.

His snowy owl smelled like *gardenia*. He wanted to breathe her in. He loved ranching, but he was in love with the sexy snowy owl.

"I want to stay, but I want to be with you more. You are everything. I love you, Griz. My owl needs your bear. I'll go with you."

Melody breathed her answer, afraid of what he would say.

"Then I will stay. I love you. As long as I have you, I'll be happy. I get so lost in you. I drown in you, and I don't even care because I *want* to drown. Will you stay here with me?"

Melody put her arms up around his neck and pulled his head down as she tiptoed up to kiss him.

Griz fell into the kiss and drowned in the love that was Melody. He kissed her long and passionately. He lost all track of time and place.

There was only Melody. Her soft lips pressed against his, and her soft body pressed against his hard muscles. Her fingers threaded through the back of his hair. The smell of *gardenia* narrowed his focus on his mate.

She broke the kiss to breathe.

"Yes, I will stay here with you."

Griz was back looking at his lifemate. Looking at Melody. Listening to applause.

Griz looked up, embarrassed. Melody blushed. Griz put his arm around her and walked toward the small crowd of people gathered on the porch.

Griz stood at the bottom step and looked up at his alpha.

"Melody wishes to stay. I will accept your offer. I'll stay and manage the ranch."

"I accept your offer. I will stay and be the pack's fashion designer and let Draoithe build me a workshop and a boutique."

Melody spoke up. She was all smiles. Griz had never been happier.

"Great, I'll be magic drunk on Sunday for sure. Come and eat, the pack ordered Chinese. Let's discuss what we need to buy. What do you want to drive, Griz? Oh, by the way, several packages arrived for you."

Luke spoke as he went into the house. Griz didn't hear him. He was too busy kissing his owl again.

CHAPTER THIRTY-ONE

Her Bear

elody

M Melody woke Wednesday morning to a happy Griz. He held an old horse's saddle in his hands as he rubbed some kind of oil into it. Melody smiled.

If Griz did something, it made him happy. He didn't enjoy sitting still unless he was in the dream. Melody looked at the clock.

It was barely six in the morning. Griz was most definitely a morning person. Melody grinned as she remembered the sitting rooms at Draoithe. She'd certainly put that to good use.

She was an owl. They were most active at night. She snuggled back down into the covers, which smelled like *baled hay in the sun.*

Griz should bottle his scent and sell it. On second thought, maybe not. She didn't like the idea of every woman sniffing his scent. That belonged to her.

She looked at him while he worked. He'd already polished his boots. She had a feeling he'd peeked in on the rabbits and chickens that morning already, too. He didn't trust the servants.

Griz was sexy. He sat in his jeans and an undershirt. His feet had socks on, but his shirt hung over the back of the chair.

She could see his arm and chest muscles shift beneath his skin as he rubbed the oil into the leather and shifted the saddle so he didn't miss a spot. The bruising had healed and only a few pink scars remained. Griz was too good to be true.

He looked up and caught her staring at him. She blushed. He grinned and went back to work.

Griz liked her watching him. He wanted her to know he knew she did it. The man had years of experience she didn't.

Griz finished and carefully set the saddle on the table next to him. He stood up and walked over to her.

"If the smell of *gardenia* gets any stronger, people will complain. I can't have that. It would ruin my reputation."

He stopped next to the bed and looked down at her.

Melody hid under the covers. Only the top of her head and her eyes were showing. Griz reached out and drew the covers away from her. He looked her over from head to toe. Melody saw him get hard as he looked at her. She swallowed.

Griz sat down on the edge of the bed and put his hand on her leg just below the hem of her blue silk nightdress. He squeezed her thigh gently with his hand. She caught her breath.

His hands were big and rough from years of outdoor manual labor. He looked at her face as he let his rough palm glide gently over the skin of her thigh.

As his hand moved closer to her sex, she became nervous. He smiled at her.

When his hand pressed against her heat, she knew he could feel the moisture soaking her panties. She wanted him, and he knew it.

He crawled. He wasn't in any hurry. The magic didn't press him. He sought her emotions through their shared link. He felt her anticipation.

Melody licked her lips as she stared back at him.

Griz pushed her panties to the side and slid his finger into her. Melody moaned at the sweet invasion. She wanted Griz. She was desperate for his touch, and he gave her what she needed.

He moved his finger in and out of her. She moaned, and her hips moved with his hand. She couldn't help herself. Just his finger inside her was causing her to spiral up toward an orgasm.

Everything about Griz was a turn-on. The way he walked. The way he dressed. His strength, his control, and his precision in whatever task made her crazy for him.

He stood up and unbuttoned and unzipped his pants with his free hand. His pants and boxers slid down to the floor with a push. He still fingered her, watching the pleasure cross her face.

He stepped out of his pants and knelt on the bed between her open legs. He drew his finger out of her and brought it to his lips. Griz licked the wet juice from his finger as his eyes slipped closed in pleasure at the way she tasted. Griz rumbled. The sound thrilled Melody.

"I need to taste your honey."

He spoke thickly, as if there were gravel in his voice.

Her panties disappeared. He tore the fabric as if it were paper.

Her honey dripped down her inner thigh. She wanted him to taste it. He dipped his head between her legs, and his tongue slid over her petals. He licked the juice off of her.

His tongue darted into her tunnel, and she felt his lips seal to hers as if he were French kissing her pussy. He sucked the honey out of her and licked her clean.

She squirmed beneath his face, but he clenched her hips.

He looked up, grinning. He had her juice on his chin.

"I want more. Don't move."

He let her hip go, and he slid his finger back into her. His finger was rough, but it was big like his hands, and not moving was torture. She tried hard to hold still, but it was an impossibility.

He stroked her with his finger, then he placed his lips on her clit. He licked her while he fingered her. Griz forced her to the edge of an orgasm and paused.

"You're going to say my name, and I'm going to drink down your pleasure. Try not to move."

Griz paused in sucking her clit to tell her.

He smiled at her, and he licked her again. His tongue swirled masterfully around her hard nub. As she climaxed, Melody repeated his name over and over, and he didn't stop.

He held her down and forced her climax to drag out as long as he could extend it. Spent and trembling, he withdrew his finger, licked it clean, and then lapped at all her honey, drinking it down.

"Oh yes, I found the honey hole."

Griz licked his lips as he looked at her.

He intended to take her. She could feel it. She had no intention of protesting.

Melody needed him. His thirst had slaked, but it only stoked his desire. He was hard for her.

Griz intended to ride her slowly for hours. He fell into her and got lost. She wanted him to do just that.

She wanted him to go slow and ride her. He positioned himself and slid into her. They rocked slowly together.

Hung like a bear, he stretched her tight around him. He glided into her, touching every part of her. She never wanted him to stop.

Being stretched and filled by Griz was perfect. She moaned out his name and came on him again.

He rode her. He had the stamina of a bear to go with his size.

She begged him to go faster. He smiled, and he stroked her faster. He lost himself to her, to his desire for her. She built up to another orgasm, and he let her fall over the edge and shatter again as he continued to stroke her.

He let her beg him for more, gave it to her, and watched her shatter over and over and over. Griz couldn't stop. He didn't want to stop.

Finally, when her body refused to clench him again in exhaustion, he gave her his strength. She begged him for that, too.

The pleasure was so intense when he slammed into her, she couldn't breathe. She trembled as he pounded her again and again until he exploded.

When he came and his cock jerked inside her, she was so swollen she felt his semen enter her. She felt it gush out of him in ropes.

"Melody, I can't make it stop," Griz rumbled in pleasure.

Griz came for three straight minutes. Melody floated so high on the euphoria of his orgasm with her there was no way she wanted to help him stop.

She drained him dry and took every ounce of his juice to replace what he drank from her. His low, reverberating rumble of pleasure made her skin tingle. It felt glorious.

Griz slumped finally and rolled to one side of her, breathing raggedly. She drained him dry and left him as completely spent as she was. His body trembled.

When she rolled to face him, he pulled up the covers and locked his arms around her. He slept lost in her. She closed her eyes and slept, too.

He would be in the barn in the dream. She went to him. Draoithe had its *Angry King* and Melody had her bear.

CHAPTER THIRTY-TWO
End Note from the Author

Ophelia Kee

Thank you for reading this last volume in the *Draoithe Saga* miniseries tales of *the Royal Council*. The pack Luke envisioned grew quickly once the threat from Peter Elliot loomed more menacing. At the end of *Angry King*, the ruling council is complete. The Druid pack had defenses in place to protect its members and aid others in need. Draoithe was on course to become more than an immortal retreat and sanctuary. A kingdom patterned on the early medieval kingdoms of Ireland meant dragons. Please accept a personal invitation to read the fantastic prophecy fueled love stories of the Valkyrie Riders. You will find a sneak peek included next.

You continue to be welcome to the dream... -OK

CHAPTER THIRTY-THREE

Sneak Peek at Raven's Rescue

A ^{sh} Damn it! Smoke would die again. That dragon had always meddled in things he should just stay out of. The damn fool had better hope Fox brought him back before he lost any memories.

If Keira was right, Griz needed to be pushed over an edge to regain himself. Ash had to let it happen. Luke wanted Griz as the seventh man on the council. Lightning would be furious if it didn't happen.

Ash stepped into the solarium to speak with Eli.

"My queen, how may I help you?"

"I need some answers. Can you explain the situation when you and the dragons met Kallik and Mihaela in the safe house?"

"Kallik is a powerful dreamwalker. When he saw all of my brothers together, he realized we had resulted from the work of a necromancer. It put him off. Flame made it worse by complimenting his vampire consort, even though that's proper etiquette for a vampire princess."

174

"Kallik roared at us. Mihaela froze all the dragons in place until Luke demanded she free us. Kallik eventually decided we were acceptable, so long as none of us looked at his mate. He put Flame in charge of Mihaela's safety and then gave his dragon to the vampire princess as a present. Mihaela has a pet dragon."

"How did Mihaela freeze the dragons?"

"My queen, she is vjestice. Her kind exists to give orders to servants. Dragons are servants. She merely thought 'freeze' at us all, and we froze."

"She took you all out with a single thought?"

Eli wanted clarification.

"Yes."

It still irritated Ash, but without his Valkyrie, he still served as a servant. Eli was curious about the weakness in dragons.

"Can anyone else do that?"

"Only vjestice and zduhaci can order dragons around like that, but not one bound to a Valkyrie. The Valkyries set dragons free. They alone can order a bonded dragon, as Mihaela did."

He didn't bother explaining how his status as Lord of the Dragons could cancel that for himself. It was a bit too complicated.

"So claiming your mate raises you from servant to what?"

Eli was curious. She was a tiger.

"I would become a free dragon. I could fly. But I would lose my invincibility to my Valkyrie. If she found me failing to maintain my oath to my Ri ruirech, she could destroy me, and I couldn't stop her. I become her great strength, and she becomes my greatest weakness."

"So you sacrifice invincibility for freedom. You place your life in the hands of your mate. If she decides to end your existence, she could order you to freeze and then kill you."

Ash nodded.

"Why would you do this?"

"I wish to fly honorably."

The answer seemed obvious to him.

"How did you fly before?"

"I swore to protect and serve my handlers."

He wouldn't deny his queen the information she sought.

"These handlers couldn't kill you as a Valkyrie could?"

"No, my queen. For a dragon to fly, a handler had to ride a dragon with whom she had a physical connection."

Ash looked at her feet. He couldn't meet his queen's gaze. Ash wouldn't see her disgust with his admission. He heard Isabell and Artie inhale, but still neither woman interrupted his and Eli's conversation.

"How many?"

"I don't understand the question, my queen."

"How many women did you service?"

"All that demanded it of me."

Eli grew silent for a long moment. Ash guessed she'd assumed it worked the other way around.

"My queen, you would know the heart of a dragon. I exist to protect the realm. I can't harm a woman or a child. In this, there can be no exception. The handlers all came to the dragons and required our service to help us do our jobs. My brothers and I suffered because we refused to turn anyone into Valkyries who weren't our lifemates. We all wanted something real, the chance at a genuine bond. The shaman made us dragons, but we each still have the soul of a man."

"Thank you, Ash. I understand now why you came. I'll help your cause if I can. Luke isn't interested in power for power's sake. If the dragons wish to join the pack, Luke will require you to be mated and bonded first. None would sanction a system of handlers. Not as I had envisioned it, nor as you have described it, could that be acceptable!"

Eli looked at Ash to ensure he understood her. She hated the idea of the riders. Ash smiled and bowed.

"Thank you, my queen. I didn't believe the Ri ruirech would treat us with the same as before. It's nice to hear you say it. My brothers and I would prefer to serve with honor and dignity."

"I suggested some of the rescued women may have skills which could benefit Draoithe. Luke wants to interview and make job offers to those who would be interested. He's not a stingy man. Will you let the other dragons know what he's doing and why? If dragons would have a proper place in the pack, then a balance had to be maintained. Luke worked hard to make all of this a reality. All the current council members equally commit themselves. Will you help make his vision a reality?"

"My queen, your wish is my command. The dragons are all working toward the same goal. We won't fail in the missions Luke has given us."

Ash smiled at Eli. His queen was on his side. Ash felt better knowing Eli wanted the same things as her mate. Serving two divergent ideals would've been difficult.

"The painting's magnificent, Isabell. It's a perfect likeness of Andrei and Nadine. You have outstanding talent. Would you consider painting the dragons?"

Ash examined the art.

"Perhaps when you mate with your Valkyrie, I'll paint the two of you." Isabell smiled.

"The time has grown short. Artie, I came here seeking Fox's help. Smoke is about to die, and I need Fox to bring him back, so he doesn't suffer memory loss in the Netherworld. The Nephilim warned me not to interfere and bring clothes for Griz and Melody. Can you assist me?" Ash requested.

Artie looked at Eli. She didn't want to respond to an unbonded male.

"What's going on?" Eli asked.

"Griz is suffering from a mental block. He could not shift on-demand perhaps because of some drug administered to him. The Nephilim has seen a way to help him. Smoke will have to die. Have no fear, it won't be the first time. Fox drowned him three times in a row once to stop the hiccups."

Ash laughed.

"Artie, go get Fox. I'll gather the clothes. Where should we meet you?"

"On this side of the little bridge that crosses the creek into the woods. In about five minutes?"

Want More From The Dream?

That you have read one of my stories is humbling to me. I sincerely hope you enjoyed your experience in the dream. Please be kind and leave an independent author an honest review. Your kind words about my stories help other readers decide to read in the dream as well and support the creative effort of one self-publishing tiger. Thank you, -OK

Magic Scroll

Join the **Newsletter** for Behind-the Scenes Updates, Exclusive Offers, Sneak Peeks, and Free Stories!

Please Safelist **opheliakee@opheliakee.com**

Newsletter Friends

Support an independent author and subscribe to **Read the Draoithe Saga** and read it all before the books publish, while I write and edit, and get all the extras, such as AI audio, character art, lexicons, graphics, videos, and more.

Read the Draoithe Saga

Visit **OpheliaKee.com** for books, audiobooks, e-boxed sets, blog posts, videos, miniseries, the suggested read order, to join the newsletter, and subscribe to Read the Draoithe Saga.

OpheliaKee.com

Welcome to the dream...

Also By Ophelia Kee

Kingdom Rising
Thread
A Pack Forms
Druid Fox
Big Bad Wolf

Royal Council
Arctic Fox
Vampire Knight
Dream Walker
Vampire Panther
Angry King

Valkyrie Riders
Coming Soon!

Druid Dominion
Still Waters

Crimson Dragon
Ruler of the Mind

Mystic Dark Prequel Trilogy
Haunted Echoes
Ruined Hearts
Shattered Souls

Acknowledgments From

OPHELIA KEE

Thanks, everyone!

I want to say thanks to my mom for always supporting me.

Thanks to my sister who has always been my first beta reader.

Thanks to my dragon for encouraging a tiger to play with books.

Thanks to my lost wolf, who provided inspiration.

Most of all, thanks to my readers who always ask the hard questions, which means I have to write more stories.

I love you, -OK

Contact Ophelia Kee

ARC READERS WANTED

Drop by and say hello!

*Email the author: **opheliakee69@gmail.com**

*Ophelia Kee on Social Media: Look for me on these sites.

**YouTube Threads Facebook
Instagram Pinterest**

I look forward to hearing from you. Sincerely, -OK

About the Author

Not who everyone thinks she is.

The product of someone's imagination.

The end result of a lifetime wishing to get out.

Do not buy the lie.

If you live in fear, you give up freedom.

Taking the risk and making the leap.

Too much of anything is a bad thing.

Innuendo floating on mist rising above water.

Walk away and leave it all behind.

Telling the story that haunts a fantasy.

Catching a dream.

She does not exist.

-Ophelia Kee

Ophelia Kee